PRAISE F(

'Original, atmospheric and beautiful –
Locked Out Lily is a perfectly-formed
tale of friendship and courage'
SARAH CROSSAN
award-winning author of *One*

'A tour de force. Genuinely scary,
wonderfully funny and held together
with a great deal of love'
SALLY GARDNER
award-winning author of *Maggot Moon*

'Beautifully written, with a powerful
undertow of emotion'
PÁDRAIG KENNY
bestselling author of *Tin*

'Utterly enchanting, a haunting
and hugely atmospheric page-turner'
LIZ HYDER
award-winning author of *Bearmouth*

First published in Great Britain in 2023 by Simon & Schuster UK Ltd

Text copyright © 2023 Nick Lake
Illustrations copyright © 2023 Emily Gravett

1 3 5 7 9 10 8 6 4 2

Simon & Schuster UK Ltd
1st Floor, 222 Gray's Inn Road
London
WC1X 8HB

www.simonandschuster.co.uk
www.simonandschuster.com.au
www.simonandschuster.co.in

Simon & Schuster Australia, Sydney
Simon & Schuster India, New Delhi

A CIP catalogue record for this book is available from the British Library.

HB 9781471194863

Printed and bound by CPI Group (UK) Ltd, Croydon, CR0 4YY

MIX
Paper | Supporting
responsible forestry
FSC® C171272

NICK LAKE

THE HOUSE WITH A DRAGON IN IT

ILLUSTRATED BY

EMILY GRAVETT

Simon & Schuster

All my books are for Hannah.
This one, in particular, is also for Lyra.
N.L.

For Rory, Tilly, Tyler, Romeo and Vinny
E.G.

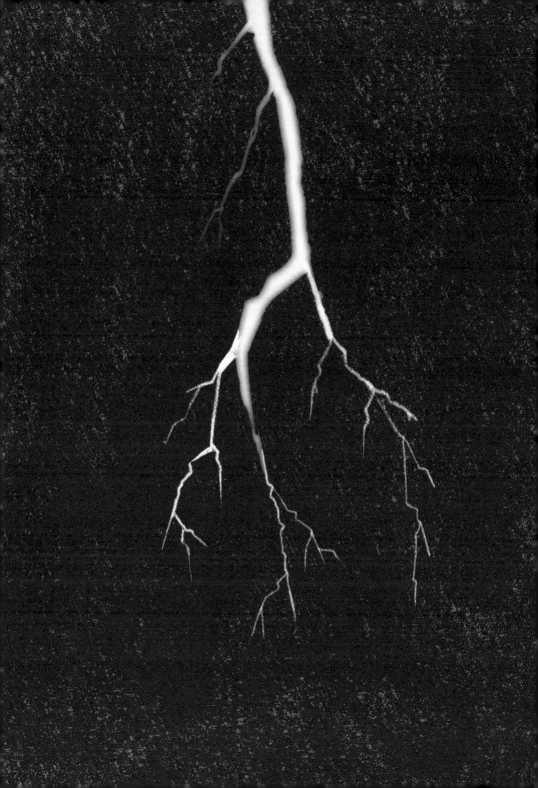

Prologue

When Summer was little, her real mum used to tell her that if she ever saw a glass bottle lying on the ground, she should not pick it up in case a witch was inside.

She said that one day Summer might know why, but she hoped not.

Chapter 1

The sinkhole opened up in the middle of Sunday lunch. In the middle of the living room, too. The hole appeared just after Summer had shouted something really loudly, almost as if her shouting had made it happen. What she shouted, precisely, to the man at the other end of the table was, 'You're not my dad!'

Which was *accurate* – Mr Pattinson was her foster father – but perhaps not *useful or kind*, as her Year Five teacher would have told her. It was, in Summer's opinion, deserved, though, seeing as Mr Pattinson wouldn't let her eat her roast beef with all the trimmings until she'd said grace, and she didn't want to say grace.

'You're not my dad!' she said, really quite loudly – and then the living-room floor fell in.

Not in a small way, either, if living rooms can even fall in different ways. No, the noise was exactly the sound of an entire room collapsing into a massive great hole in the ground that hadn't been there a moment before. Which is to say, it was loud.

They all got up from the table and rushed through to the living room in a tangle of limbs. Summer bashed into one of the Original Children, Oscar, or he bashed into her more likely. She almost tripped when the littler Original Child, Ethan, got under her feet in his haste to see the damage.

They all stood and stared.

For once, Mrs Pattinson had nothing to say. (Mrs Pattinson always had quite a lot to say and, when Summer had shouted, was opening her mouth, presumably to say quite a lot about politeness, when the living room turned into a crater.)

'Um . . .' said Mr Pattinson, which was actually something *he* said quite a lot.

Summer had pointed this out once, in what she thought was a reasonable response to him laughing about how much she supposedly said 'like', and it turned out Not To Be Polite. Mrs Pattinson had strong views about what was polite and what wasn't.

'That's a big hole,' said Oscar. (Who could be relied upon to make the observation so obvious and stupid that no one

else would bother to make it.)

'Where's the TV?' said Ethan. (Who liked watching TV.)

'It's, like, in the big hole,' said Summer because she knew it would annoy Mr Pattinson.

But Mr Pattinson wasn't paying attention. He was just looking at the huge great enormous hole where the living room had been. It was big, and deep, and steep-sided, and if you peered down into it – which Summer did – you got an impression of moisture, and blackness, and a sort of raw chasm that didn't belong in a house. There was a lot of jagged-looking rock.

The sofa had fallen into it, and the coffee table, and the armchairs, and the unit with the TV on it. Bears, too.

Mrs Pattinson was one of those people who collected things. Someone had once given her a bear figurine, and then everyone thought she liked them, and kept getting them for Christmas or birthday presents, until she had dozens, in different sizes, materials and colours. Summer knew that she didn't like them because Mrs Pattinson would often say, 'I don't even like bears very much.' By some grown-up logic for grown-ups, though, it seemed she couldn't simply *tell* people this. Perhaps it would Not Be Polite.

Now the bears were in the hole, existing in a new world of rock and water.

Summer knew how they felt. Her life had always been a thing out of place. Her life was a mole, blind and blinking in the daylight; it was a woolly jumper shrunk in the wash so it didn't fit right; it was people saying to her *home is where the heart is*, and yet her heart was right there with her, in her chest, all the time. And it wasn't. Ever. Home.

Mr Pattinson had taken his phone out of his pocket. 'I'll, um, phone the insurance company,' he said.

'It's Sunday,' said Mrs Pattinson. 'They won't be open.'

'But it's an emergency.'

'Yes,' she said. 'And you didn't get the twenty-four-hour seven-day-a-week home emergency cover, remember? You said it was too expensive. Because of the house being so old.'

The way she said this – which was the way she said many things, or at least so it seemed to Summer – made it both a statement and an accusation.

'Um . . .'

'Do you think the potatoes are getting cold?' asked Oscar. Oscar was a growing boy – that was what his parents said.

'Oscar!' said his mother.

'What? There's a big hole, I know. But it's still lunchtime.'

So they went back to the kitchen, except for Ethan and Summer. Ethan only came up to Summer's waist, and she rather liked him.

'Deep,' he said, looking at the hole.

'Yes,' she said.

'Like you.'

She turned to him, startled. 'What do you mean?'

He shrugged. 'I don't know. But it's true.' Then he turned and ran into the kitchen.

Summer followed.

And, for the rest of the day, she kept following – following the rules, following the chart for her chores, following the meal plan. Because she was afraid it had been her, shouting, that had made the hole open up. Because she was afraid she was difficult – a thing out of place – and that was why people didn't want her. Mothers.

Every time she passed the hole, all afternoon, she was drawn to look at it, down into its depths. It felt to her – and this was why Summer was worried about her shouting – that in some way she didn't quite understand it was *for* her.

That it was waiting for her.

Chapter 2

Summer's school uniform was itchy. It was the first new, not-hand-me-down school uniform she'd had, which she had to admit to being a bit grateful for, but the cotton hadn't softened and settled yet, and it clung uncomfortably in places.

She wasn't paying much attention to it, though: she was standing as quietly as she could, so as not to get in the way. The woman from the council, plus the builder Mr Pattinson knew from when they'd had the house done up, as well as the insurance-appointed surveyor man, were looking at the hole. Occasionally, the surveyor man, peering down, would tut or click his tongue.

'I'll say it again,' he said. 'This hole isn't right.'

'You *can* say that again,' said Mrs Pattinson. 'It's in the middle of our living room.'

The man tutted again. He wore an ill-fitting blue suit with no tie, and had a pen in his breast pocket.

'It just shouldn't be here,' he said. 'This is oolitic limestone – all the way down, it looks like. There's no evidence of a water table – no signs of subsidence or mud. No cracking to the rest of the room. It's just . . . a huge hole in the rock. It's as if it's always been here.'

'Well, it hasn't,' said Mr Pattinson dryly. 'I think we'd have noticed.'

Summer smiled, despite herself. He could be quite funny.

'Can you fill it in?' said Mrs Pattinson, looking at the surveyor, then the builder. 'With concrete or something?'

'Aw man,' said the builder. 'That's a ruddy big hole, that is, pet. I cannae fill that wi' concrete. Best case, you put a slab on it, but even then you'd have to dig the whole room out to nearly a metre and do the insulation an' that. It's regulation.'

Except he didn't say 'ruddy'; he said another worse word, and after that he glanced at Summer and mumbled an apology. Mrs Pattinson glared at him.

'Indeed,' said the woman from the council. 'Insulation, membrane, all of that.'

'I've never seen anything like it,' said the insurance

surveyor, looking at the hole. 'I'll have to talk to the company. See what they say. It'll be a considerable job, and the question of liability . . . I mean, one wonders if the wooden floor was put over it, back in the day.'

'You're saying someone put a house on top of a massive hole and just . . . covered it up?' said Mr Pattinson.

'These old houses, they contain all sort of horrors,' said the surveyor.

Summer shivered a little. Was she imagining a chill breeze coming from the hole?

'Do you have anything else to say?' said Mrs Pattinson to the woman from the council.

'I'll need to speak to my superiors,' she said.

'Wonderful,' said Mr Pattinson. 'So, in the meantime, we have to live with the hole?'

'You should erect some sort of fencing,' said the surveyor. 'Don't want a child falling in there. It's deep.'

'Ah can do that for you, like,' said the builder. 'Cheaper than filling it in.'

'One would hope so,' said Mr Pattinson.

They kept discussing it for a little while, in those hushed tones that adults use when they're cross, but won't show it, and Summer peered at the hole while they talked. She was quite glad all these people were here – it meant she'd been able to get into the house right after school, rather than waiting for it to be unlocked. Or going to After-school Club, which was something she would basically eat her own toes before doing. Deep down, at the bottom of the rock sides of the hole, she thought she saw a glimmer of light, but then it was gone.

She didn't know what oolitic meant, or whatever the surveyor man had said, but she sort of knew what he was getting at: there was something *geological* about the hole. Like a textbook illustration; a cut-away diagram that said *rock* and *old*. Not old like the house, but much, much older.

After five minutes or so, with no conclusion about the hole and who was going to pay for it or what to do with it, the adults – apart from Mr and Mrs Pattinson – left, and soon after that the door banged open, and Oscar and Ethan were back, dropped off by other parents after football or violin or whatever it was they'd been doing.

They raced into the living room, dropping their stuff, and gazed excitedly at the hole.

'Slow down!' said Mrs Pattinson, from where she was

closing the front door after them. 'You'll fall in.'

'It's still there,' said Oscar.

Summer rolled her eyes at him, but he didn't see.

'It'll be staying,' said Mr Pattinson, coming into the room, 'if the surveyor is to be believed. And the builder.'

'*Really?*' said Ethan.

'Well, I really hope not,' said Mr Pattinson. 'But Rick doesn't know what to do with it.'

'Rick said that?' said Oscar. 'When he did the extension, he was always telling you what had to be done.'

Mr Pattinson coughed, lightly. 'Well, he didn't exactly say he didn't *know* what to do, but he didn't quite have a solution, either.'

'Oh. So what *did* he—'

'He said,' said Summer, remembering the man's accent, '*Haway, man, that's a big hole, pet. I cannae fill that.*'

She did it without thinking. People's voices – some people's anyway – had always got inside her. As if the sound came in through her ears and stayed in her head, moving around. Like butterflies. And she could open her mouth and let them out.

Mr Pattinson laughed, surprised. 'That was spot on,' he

said. 'Not exactly what he said, but very impressive.'

Mrs Pattinson was looking cross. 'We don't swear in this house, Summer,' she said.

'I—' began Summer, but Oscar was looking at her, wide-eyed, and Ethan was pulling on her arm.

'Do Dad!' he said. 'Do Dad!'

Summer glanced at Mr Pattinson, who nodded, smiling. Summer still felt like this might make him angry, but he was telling her to do it, right?

'Can you . . . say something?' she said. 'Anything. Talk about football, or work, or something.'

Mr Pattinson spoke for a few seconds about golf. Summer wasn't really paying attention to the words, but to the sounds in them. He hadn't grown up here; not in England. There was another song under his breath, a different tune to the vowels. Wales? He had also lived, she thought, somewhere further away for a bit, or his parents had. She got most of her knowledge from TV, and she thought this had a hint of . . . not Australia. New Zealand, maybe?

Whatever it was – she felt it settle, with the other parts of his voice, into a compact shape. The butterflies opened their wings.

'*Clean your room, boys,*' she said, facing Ethan and Oscar. '*And be snappy about it.*' Going deep in timbre, letting a bit of song in, a bit of a different light, from the other side of the world.

Oscar and Ethan laughed, delighted.

Mrs Pattinson even forced a little smile. 'On that note, I'd better get back to work,' she said. 'You all right to cook, darling?'

Mr Pattinson nodded and followed her into the kitchen, saying something about leftover roast beef.

Oscar turned to Summer and gave her a high five, and then he and Ethan left the room, too, chattering about a goal one of them had scored. Definitely football.

Summer stayed and looked at the hole for a bit.

The hole stayed, too. That day – and for several days afterwards.

The insurance company called and said they couldn't do anything about it because it was an 'act of God', which Summer thought was ironic given all the saying of grace that went on in the house.

Mr Pattinson got some police-line-do-not-cross tape from somewhere, and strung it across the living-room door while they waited for Rick to come and put up some proper fencing. Summer wasn't sure where he'd found it – Mr Pattinson wasn't a police officer. He was a civil engineer, whatever that was. Summer thought it sounded like an engineer could fill the hole in, but when she said this he laughed, and said not that kind.

In time, Summer almost got used to the hole – despite the weird pull it had on her, the way it made her want to look deep into it, to where that spark of light had seemed to appear, washing the limestone red. She learned to ignore it – the way the rest of the family seemed to do quite naturally.

Until the night she was getting a glass of water from the kitchen, and the hole began to smoke, in the narrow, conical depths, and a voice from far down inside it spoke to her.

DO NOT CROSS   DO NOT CROSS

Chapter 3

The voice didn't speak *to* her, exactly. It wasn't like it said Summer's name or anything.

But it spoke.

'Who disturbs my slumber?' it said. It was a low voice; gravelly. As if it hadn't been used for some time.

Summer blinked, standing in the dark of the doorway, lit only by the green light from the flashing clocks in the kitchen ahead of her, telling different times.

'I *said*: who disturbs my slumber?'

This was the kind of thing Mr Pattinson would say as a joke if the Original Children woke him up by playing too loudly on a Saturday morning. But it didn't sound like a joke, coming from a dark, smoking hole in the ground. It sounded really, really scary.

Summer took a step back.

'What's that noise?' said the voice from the hole in the living room. 'What manner of creature are you?'

'I'm a person,' said Summer.

'Begone, person. Disturb me no more,' said the voice.

'I'm going. And I'm not disturbing you. At least not deliberately. I'm getting some water.'

'A coward's trick! If you want the treasure, you face me with steel edge and iron shield, not with water.'

'What?' said Summer.

Then she paused.

Treasure?

If you'd been in as many foster homes as Summer, treasure became a magic word. Treasure wasn't just gold coins buried by a pirate, or jewels locked in a castle, it was anything special, something all of your own, something you guarded. Summer didn't have much like that, apart from bits of her, deep down inside, that she kept for herself and shared with no one. Christmas presents were usually books, clothes that didn't quite fit. Nothing terribly personal. Once, she'd had a soft toy, an elephant, that her real mum gave her. But she'd lost it, somehow, in one of her moves.

'What treasure?' she said, eventually.

The voice was silent.

Then, after a moment: 'Forget I said that.'

Summer thought, *Treasure sounds interesting.* There wasn't a lot in her life that was interesting.

Slowly, she approached the hole. There was a glimmer of red light coming from the depths, and that steady trickle of smoke. The voice had gone quiet again, but there was a sort of rumble, like something large was moving. But Summer wasn't scared – or at least she wasn't as scared as much as interested. She had been in bad houses where bad things happened. Going down into a big hole in the ground wasn't like that: wasn't like grown-ups doing things and deciding things. It was *her* deciding.

Even if it was a stupid idea.

Summer glanced around. She didn't have her own phone, otherwise she'd have used it as a torch. She wished she *did* have her own phone. Then she could message Aishwarya about this. Though she wasn't sure what Aishwarya would say. She'd told her best friend at school about the living room, the day after it happened, and how she was worried she'd made the hole herself, by shouting.

'Maybe you can come and shout in my brother's room,'

Aishwarya had said, with a laugh. 'It would be easier than persuading him to tidy it.'

Now Summer went into the kitchen. She wasn't thirsty any more, but she got herself a glass of water, anyway – there was something hot-looking about that red light down in the hole. Then she searched in the kitchen drawers until she found a torch, hidden at the back of the one where bits of old candle and string and batteries were kept. She clicked it on – and it worked.

Carrying the torch, she went back to the living room and approached the hole. Summer had never climbed down into a sinkhole before. Obviously. And she wasn't quite sure how to go about it. But sometimes you just had to get on with things. She clamped the torch in her teeth – it was a narrow LED one with grippy rubber casing – and sat on the edge. She could swear there was a warmth, a kind of breeze, coming from below. She turned herself around, so she could lower her legs backwards into the hole, and slowly, she eased herself down. She was in pyjamas that were slightly too small, hand-me-downs from an Original Child, and the edges of the living room floor scraped at her elbows and knees.

But then her feet found a ledge, or something ledge-like,

and she paused before lowering herself again. It helped that the hole was roughly conical: wider at the top, and tapering to a narrower point. Maybe it would just end there, and she'd have to climb back out again.

Her foot slipped – and she bashed and scraped against the earth and rock as she skidded down, yelping, until she caught an old rusted pipe that was sticking out and swung there, grabbing with her other hand, too.

Summer looked down. Her feet were only a metre or so from the bottom. Wincing and briefly closing her eyes, she let go.

Bang.

She hit the ground and crumpled, then righted herself, leaning against the wall. She rubbed at her sore arms. Then she took the torch from her mouth and spun gently on the spot, aiming the beam of light at the sides of the sinkhole. It was damp down here and cold – Summer didn't know why she'd thought there was a warmth coming from it – and there was a smell of earthy mulch and, faintly, acrid sulphur.

She stopped.

Turning round, she saw a low tunnel disappearing into darkness, like an iris with a pupil of blackness in the middle.

From that blackness came the voice.

'Are you coming then, hero?' it said.

Chapter 4

Summer wasn't giving up now, even if she was scared. Even if she wasn't, at all, a hero.

She put the torch back in her mouth and got down on her hands and knees, then crawled into the tunnel. Earth crumbled as her back scraped against it, falling round her, granular, with a sound like rain. Every so often, there were wooden struts, and narrow beams overhead, like in an old mine. At one point, Summer raised her head, just at the wrong moment, and smacked it against one, swearing under her breath. It was cold down here.

The red light got brighter.

And, as it got brighter, the tunnel widened – almost imperceptibly at first, but then obviously, and soon her back wasn't touching the soil any more, and just after that she was on her feet.

Summer walked forward, into a cavern.

She stopped, and her mouth opened, and the torch fell out, bouncing on the rock floor. But she didn't need it any more.

She didn't need it because of the glow coming from the dragon's mouth, and its eyes, and the torches flickering on the wall.

Summer blinked.

Yes. Yes, that really was a *dragon*. She felt her fingers trembling.

The air was warmer here, a breeze on her skin. The smell of sulphur was stronger in the air. The dragon was enormous: curled in the corner of the cavern, it nevertheless took up most of it, a huge reticulated mass of scales and claws, ending in that vast head, with its colossal jaws. Above the teeth, two nostrils, each the size of Summer herself, smoking.

'Are you ready?' said the dragon.

'Ready for . . . w-w-what?' stammered Summer.

'To fight me. For the treasure.'

'What treasure? I can't see any.'

Fire snorted from those big nostrils. 'The treasure I am guarding, of course. Are you a child?'

'Yes,' said Summer.

The dragon blinked, this time. Great hoods came down over its vast lizard eyes, their flickering, flaming depths, and then rose. 'I see. You are very brave. That is a pity.'

Summer chose not to let the implications of that sink too far into her.

'What am I meant to fight you with?'

'There is a weapon, if you are worthy to wield it,' said the dragon.

Its barbed tail lifted from the ground and indicated a large stone, to Summer's left, with a sword sticking out of it.

'A sword in a stone?' said Summer. 'That's a bit of a cliché, isn't it?'

'Everything is merely what it is,' said the dragon in its low voice, a voice like boulders grinding down a mountainside.

Summer looked at the sword. She thought of the stories of Arthur, the once and future king who one day would rise again. He had pulled a sword from a stone and proved he was the one – the rightful ruler. Or sometimes a woman in a lake gave it to him. Summer thought that would be easier, on balance, than the option that involved *pulling it out of a rock*.

Now that Summer was looking at the sword, she

couldn't help but notice the other things lying around near it. Well, not things. Remains. Skeletons, of knights and other sorts of men. All men.

And something else disturbing: on the wall, close to where she stood, was the pale silhouette of a man, arms up – outlined by black soot. Like someone had been burned in an instant from the world. Erased.

Some of the bodies were skeletons; some were blackened and burnt. Others just had bits missing – as if the heat of the fire had simply subtracted limbs and heads.

'Better move quickly,' said the dragon.

And it began to uncurl, its head stretching towards her – a bus length away, but mounted on rippling scaled muscles, liquid in its progress.

Oh no.

Summer scrambled towards the sword, and tripped, and landed hard on her knees in front of it, pain shivering through her bones. She had to act fast; she had no time to process the fact that she was *underneath* the house with a *dragon*. She didn't really even have a say in what her body was doing. She reached out her hands – she could see the dragon coming, see its mouth opening – and she gripped the sword pommel and yanked and—

—it came out of the stone.

From her knees, Summer fell on her bum with a gasp. She was aware that some part of her was hoping that this was a dream, but a bigger part of her knew – just knew – that it wasn't.

'How unexpected,' said the dragon, in a puzzled tone, and for a moment it stopped moving.

Summer's heart was a spinning top: turning wildly but somehow keeping going. The sword was long and heavy, and she heaved it up so the point was facing away from her; that was the basic principle, right?

She cast her eyes around. The skeleton knight nearest her had a shield, and she launched herself sideways, tore it from his bone-fingers and shoved her arm through the two leather straps, so it was tight against her.

She whirled, sword scraping on the ground, to face the coming dragon – and it *roared*. Fire surged towards her, a boiling red cloud of it, and instinctively she held up the shield, crouching behind it. She felt burning heat roil past her on either side, smelled her hair singing, the awful bitter stench of it.

Wildly, she poked with the sword round the side of the shield and felt the dragon withdraw into the open space of the cavern.

'What is *happening*?' she spat. 'I can't use a sword. This cannot be real.'

'Maybe it isn't,' said the dragon. 'Maybe it's all an enchantment meant to guard the treasure. Maybe I'm nothing more than a spell. Just words whispered on the wind.'

'So . . . I can't die?' Because it had felt, when the fire whooshed over her, like she could.

'Oh no,' the dragon said, almost sadly. 'You can die.'

Then, with a motion that engaged its whole body, scales rippling in the red light, the dragon came rushing towards her, massive and unstoppable as a train, and it opened its mouth wide, teeth like daggers gleaming top and bottom.

No fire came this time – only the freighted power of a room-sized monster bearing down on her, and its mouth opened even wider, and Summer pushed the sword up, shield hanging uselessly as she put both hands desperately on the handle, but it was too late.

The dragon's mouth closed, with her inside it.

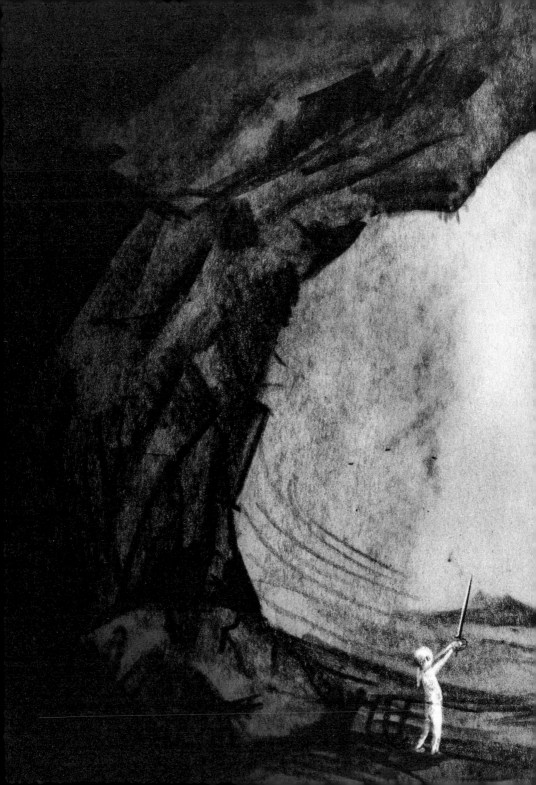

Chapter 5

The teeth didn't close on her – Summer braced for impact, for being impaled, and nothing came.

Opening her eyes, she saw she was crouching just inside the dragon's teeth, hot breath flowing round her. Holding its jaws open, filigreed iron handle against its bottom teeth and point pressing into the roof of its mouth, was the sword. Summer's hand was still on it and, experimentally, she eased open her fingers. And the sword stayed where it was, locking the giant creature's maw in a wide, painful rictus.

Tentatively, she stepped back, over the teeth, and out into the cavern.

The dragon regarded her balefully with its big eyes.

Summer took another step back.

It raised its foreclaws and tried to reach the sword, to pluck it out, but its legs were too short. It twisted, huffing smoke from its nostrils, scratching at itself. But the sword stayed stuck there. Eventually it went still, and continued glaring at her. It clearly couldn't bite down on the sword: the blade would simply push up, into its skull.

'You want me to take out the sword?' said Summer, still feeling dizzy with terror, but noticing that her hands had stopped shaking.

The dragon nodded.

Summer frowned. 'Will you give me the treasure if I do?'

A long silence.

Then the dragon nodded again, slowly.

'How do I know you won't burn me after?'

The dragon simply looked at her, and Summer thought she understood: there was another option, and it was to walk away, to climb back up into the living room, and leave the dragon down here, and the treasure, too. If she wanted to take the treasure, she had to take the risk.

On the other hand, if the dragon wanted the sword out . . .

Summer went over to the light of one of the torches, burning in the wall. She felt cold again, all of a sudden, and she shrank round the centre of herself. It was a thing she'd known how to do since she was little: make herself small. From somewhere far away, she could hear a trickle of water, as if an underwater stream were somewhere on the other side of the rock.

'I could just leave you here,' she said. 'Or I could help you, and then you give me the treasure. But you have to promise I won't get hurt after.'

The dragon shook its head.

'Fine, I'm going then.'

But the dragon shook its head again, more insistently this time, and opened its eyes wide, holding her gaze. Unfolding a front leg, it tried to block her way. Like it was trying to tell her something.

Summer thought back over what she'd said. Maybe promises were a big deal? That was the way the dragon was acting; that was written in the coils of its body. So . . .

What had been her precise words?

So . . . maybe it couldn't promise that she *wouldn't get hurt* because that wasn't entirely in its power.

'Do you promise that *you* won't hurt me after?' she said.

The dragon's eyes shone, like moonlight on metal, and it nodded.

Summer stood there in her pyjamas, in a cavern of rock lit by flaming torches, in front of a dragon that would make her school look small. Her legs were a little wobbly. But she stood firm. She shrugged. Then she approached, and seized the sword with both hands. Gently, as gently as she could, she tugged to the side, trying to free it. At the same time, she felt a straining, a vibration all around her, as the dragon forced its jaws open, wide as they would go.

With a slick slashing sound that made Summer's stomach contract, the blade swung, suddenly, and it was all she could do to keep holding on to the sword as it twisted out.

She leaped back, holding it up, as the dragon arched its neck, shaking its head, hissing steam from its nose, blinking in pain.

'Thank you,' it said.

'The treasure?' said Summer.

Did the dragon smile?

'A promise from a dragon is a promise written in fire,' said the dragon. 'The treasure is yours.'

'Written in *fire*?' said Summer, who felt slightly hysterical. 'I mean, stone I could understand, but fire . . . What if the fire goes out? Or someone comes along with a bucket of water? It doesn't seem like it's a very—'

'Do you want the treasure or not?' said the dragon.

'Yes.'

A flare of red breath. 'The same goes for a promise written in stone, by your reasoning,' it said, grumpily after a moment. 'What if someone comes along with a hammer and chisel?'

Summer thought about this. 'True.'

The dragon sighed. 'Here,' it said.

Its massive bulk shifted, scales whispering against scales, and its tail uncurled and snaked towards Summer, and she took an involuntary step backwards, but then the tail stopped. The very tip of it was wrapped round a small object, something shiny and smooth.

'Catch,' said the dragon.

Its tail unrolled, and there was a bottle standing in the air – then falling.

Summer reached out, quick as a startled bird, and caught it, holding it close. It was an old bottle – maybe very old. Blue glass shaped like a teardrop, but with a flat base, and sealed with wax.

Inside there was nothing.

'This doesn't look like treasure to me,' said Summer.

'You, who are a foundling just like me, think that what is precious is visible to the eye?'

'How do you know I—'

But she shut up. It was a dragon in a magic cave under the house. Of course it knew. And anyway it was right: what was precious, in Summer's mind, what would be treasure, was not a great pile of gold. It was things you couldn't weigh: a hand on her hair; a song sung by a bedside; a laugh; talking together all the lazy length of a long summer's day. Two eyes the exact same shade of green as hers.

Three words.

Three words she had not heard – not for half her life – not since she was little.

'What is inside that bottle can give you everything you ever wanted,' said the dragon.

Something caught Summer's eye: a label. She lifted the bottle higher.

On the label was written:

Contaynes one Witch.
DO NOT OPEN

Summer stared. She thought of what her mum used to say when she was a little girl. Had she dreamed something? Been told something about a witch in a bottle?

'Now go,' said the dragon, lumbering back to its corner. 'Before I change my mind.'

'But you promised.'

'I did. But I'm also *very* hungry.'

Summer didn't need telling twice. She turned. She stared.

The stone, which the sword had been in, the skeletons, the armour – they were all gone. There was only a bare cave. She spun, to see if she dragon was still there.

He was. Breathing out fire.

She pivoted, and ran, out of the cavern and back down the tunnel. After a moment's hesitation, she left the sword just out of sight of anyone in the living room above, inside the entrance to the tunnel.

It was only as she was climbing back up, out of the hole, the bottle tucked into her pyjama top, that Summer thought of something.

The dragon hadn't wanted to say she wouldn't come to harm.

Which meant it thought she might.

Chapter 6

After school the next day, Aishwarya fell into step beside Summer, as she always did. They had never spoken about why this was. About how the other kids used to throw stones at Summer as she walked home, until Aishwarya – who was popular – just appeared one day and kept by her side. But it was there, an awareness of it, between them.

Summer had hoped, briefly, that it would lead to more friendships, more of the children at school accepting her, but apparently it didn't work like that. Aishwarya was enough to stop stones, was a shield, but she wasn't a gateway.

'What're you thinking about?' said Aishwarya. She was kicking a fallen apple along the gutter with the Doc Martens she wasn't really meant to wear, but which she somehow got away with. 'You're all distant.'

'Oh, nothing,' said Summer. *She was thinking about the*

bottle, with the witch in it. 'I had a weird dream last night, that's all.' *Except it wasn't a dream. The bottle was under the recycling box in the front garden.*

'I have a dream,' said Aishwarya, 'about Mrs Myer quitting as head teacher and us getting a new head teacher who doesn't make us listen to handbells and stories in assembly.'

'I like story time!' said Summer. 'I can take or leave the handbells, though, I've gotta say.'

'You like the stories because you're a geek.'

'And you're a hypocrite,' said Summer. 'We first met at the *library.* Where you were hanging out on your own. And I've seen the books in your bag, remember? That whole act won't work with me.'

'Okay, fine, but the stories at school always have magic and stuff in them. I don't like that.' Aishwarya kicked the apple again and it fragmented into sections. 'I like the real world.'

They paused at the end of Summer's road, and she glanced at the house-that-was-not-her-house. It had black wooden beams and white walls, the oldest house on the street by far. The foster parents were very keen on something called 'character', which as far as Summer could see meant having ice on the inside of the windows in winter, and flagstone floors that the Original Children had tripped on when they were little, leaving scars on their foreheads.

'That's because the real world is a nice place, for you.'

Aishwarya blinked. This was as close as anything had come to an open statement of the differences between them.

'I . . .' she began. Then she sighed. 'Whatever. I get it. But I still like real stories. Classics.'

Summer wanted to say that all stories are real stories. Even when they have magic in them. Especially when they have magic in them. But she didn't. Nor did she tell Aishwarya about the dragon, or the bottle – partly because she wasn't sure how. She knew the story would make her sound crazy, and she was on thin enough ice at school as it was. Especially since she was meant to be at After-school Club right now, and didn't especially want anyone telling the Pattinsons she wasn't.

'You good from here?' said Aishwarya. 'Got to get home to help Mum with dinner.'

Aishwarya had a little brother, and was often roped into babysitting.

'Yep,' said Summer.

She couldn't get into the house when the family weren't home – she hadn't been given a key – but that wasn't Aishwarya's problem and Summer had never really mentioned it. What Aishwarya was doing was enough. Summer would find something to occupy the time until her foster parents got back from work, and the Original Children got back from their clubs and stuff. Maybe the library, or visiting Mrs Cardle or Mr Rowntree, her two elderly friends who lived in the town and loved company.

Actually – not the library. It was shut on a Wednesday. But yes, maybe tea at Mrs Cardle's, who liked to bake a Battenberg on a Tuesday, or . . .

. . . *or opening the bottle.*

It was as if the thought came from somewhere outside Summer, like a breeze.

And then it carried her, wind-like, down the road and in through the front gate. Aishwarya had gone round the corner; they'd waved to each other. Had they? Something funny had happened to time.

Summer lifted the recycling box and took out the bottle. Was that a wisp of milky white inside now? Curling, curdling.

No – just the late afternoon light filtering through the glass.

She twisted the wax seal, and it cracked easily, and as she pulled a short cork came out soundlessly.

And it was night.

Summer looked up, frantic – but it was just a dark cloud, covering the sun. She breathed out as the moving air blew it into pieces, and the pale glow returned to the sky.

In front of her was a woman, dressed like she was an exhibit in a museum. Partly because it really was a *dress*, of the kind you didn't see much outside the TV screen. It had a white frilly underneath part, and then a sort of separate leather jacket, tied with string of some kind. And over *that* was a shawl, and under it were practical boots, laced tight. And the hat. People didn't wear hats much any more. Definitely not ones like that. Pointy ones.

'You let me out,' said the woman, cocking her head to one side.

Her accent was strange. Not regionally strange. Just . . . unplaceable. Sort of Midlands, but weird. It had an otherworldly feel to it, and Summer didn't think she'd be able to copy it, not with a hundred years of training.

'You must be very brave.'

'I . . . don't think so,' said Summer.

'Nevertheless,' said the woman, as if that concluded something, 'here we are.' She stretched, as if waking. There was a click of bones. 'Thank you,' she said. 'I have been confined a long time.'

Summer was focusing on the woman's face so as not to focus on the screaming inside herself. She – the woman – had sharp cheekbones and a dainty nose; brown eyes that were almost black. She wasn't precisely pretty, but she wasn't precisely not, either.

'Are you . . . a witch?' Summer said.

'Oh no,' said the woman.

'No?'

'No. I *was* a witch. Now I'm the spirit of a witch.'

'Oh.' Summer took a step back.

'Now where is that . . . ah.'

A black cat leaped from the bottle, forming from smoke in the air, and landed at the woman's feet.

'Tobias!' she said. The cat wound round her ankles.

'Smells awful strange here,' said the cat.

Summer looked down at him. 'The cat spoke,' she said flatly.

'Oh yes,' said the witch. 'He didn't do that when we were alive. But death brings great change, I warrant.'

'Death brings boredom,' said the cat. 'What *is* that smell? Something nacreous, and unpleasant.'

The witch sniffed. 'Something burning . . . ?' she said.

Summer looked around. There was nothing obvious, and she didn't know what *nacreous* meant, anyway. Then she noticed the cars going past; the bus waiting at the stop just down the road.

'It's the engines,' she said. 'I think. From the cars.'

The witch nodded. 'People always were too clever for their own good,' she said. Then she cracked her knuckles. 'Well then,' she said. 'What manner of magic can I perform for you?'

'I'm sorry?'

'You freed me. And I am a witch. So I ask again: what manner of magic can I perform for you?'

'I . . . don't know?'

The witch shook her head. 'Lack of ambition,' she said. 'Never a fault of mine, though of course I paid for that. Go to bed and sleep on it. Tomorrow I will perform miracles for you. But my patience is not endless.'

Summer looked at her watch. 'It's four o'clock,' she said. 'It's not bedtime.'

'Then go inside, and do your needlework like a good girl.'

'People don't . . . do needlework any more.'

'Really? Well, that's an improvement, at least,' said the witch. 'What do you do, at this hour, when there is still light in the sky?'

'Not much,' said Summer. 'I don't have a key. For the house.'

She could go to After-school Club, of course. The Pattinsons weren't monsters. But – well. She didn't want to.

The witch turned to the house, and for a second she seemed to shrink into herself, as if she was made of wool, and someone had just cinched her threads tight. The cat mewed, pitifully.

'Are you all right?' said Summer.

'Perfectly,' said the witch. She stepped forward and put her hand on the handle, and the door sprang open.

'There,' she said. 'A simple spell of opening.'

Conscious of being polite, Summer paused at the threshold. 'Would you . . . like to come in?' she said.

'Into that house? Not for all the gold in Christendom,' said the witch.

Summer didn't know what Christendom was, but she guessed it had a lot of gold. 'Okay,' she said.

'I'll be back for you tomorrow,' said the witch. 'Think of what you might wish for before then. If you could do magic. Which I can.'

With that, she disappeared, and the cat, too – one instant they were there and the next they were gone.

Summer stood, holding the door for a moment. She hesitated – and then realized why. If she went in, if she was waiting inside, when the foster parents came back, they would wonder how; they might get to thinking she could break and enter, that she might steal. It had happened to her before, when she'd known that the spare key was kept under a plant pot, in a previous house.

She shut the door and went back out on to the street.

Maybe Mrs Cardle would have cake.

Chapter 7

The next day, after Aishwarya had walked her home, Summer looked for the witch, but didn't see anything, or anyone, outside the house. Just the little front garden, with the raised beds covered in moss, and the damp earth strewn with dead leaves.

She'd put the little blue bottle back under the recycling box – now she took it out, dug a hole in the soil and buried it, covering it in mud and leaves, so no one could see it. She wanted to know where it was; that it wouldn't disturbed. She wasn't sure why.

She couldn't go to Mrs Cardle's again, and Mr Rowntree wasn't in when she knocked at the door, so she headed to the library – there was something she wanted to ask, anyway. Turning right at the end of her road, Summer walked up the high street. The metal outer gate with the books etched into it was hanging open; she went inside and through the smaller door.

'Hello, Summer!' said Mrs Brathwaite, the librarian, from behind her desk. She was small and indeterminately middle-aged and packed with energy, like a neutron star.

'Hi,' said Summer.

'Aishwarya okay?' said Mrs Brathwaite. 'I haven't seen her for a while.'

'Er . . . yeah,' said Summer. 'She just walked m— I mean, we just walked home.'

'Sweet girl,' said Mrs Brathwaite. 'I always feel for her, rather, given the circumstances. By the way, your books came in. Got them on the shelf behind me.'

She bustled about, fetching the books, then stamping Summer's card, until Summer forgot the odd little comment about Aishwarya.

Summer took the books and settled in one of the armchairs in the kids' corner to read for a while. She'd spent practically the whole winter here, when it was often cold or raining, reading. Mrs Brathwaite was always kind, and didn't ask too many questions. Summer liked that.

Summer had a question, though.

After her first chapter, she put the book down on the arm of her chair and went over to the desk.

'Mrs Brathwaite,' she said.

'You can call me Val,' said the librarian.

'Okay,' said Summer. Mrs Brathwaite always said that, but Summer wasn't going to call her Val. It didn't seem right. 'Listen . . .'

'Yes?'

'Have you ever heard of . . . um . . . a witch in a bottle?'

Mrs Brathwaite's eyes gleamed behind her round glasses. 'Ah!' she said. 'The god in chains.'

'Sorry?'

'The title of an essay, I think. Or something like it. The binding of powerful entities. Why do you ask?'

Summer often didn't know what Mrs Brathwaite was talking about. 'Something I saw in a book,' she said. *And that my mum used to say*, she didn't add.

'All the best things are to be found in books,' said Mrs Brathwaite. 'Apart from Gregory Peck.'

'What?'

'Never mind.'

'What's . . . what's the binding of powerful . . . whatever you said?' said Summer.

'Oh – deities tied down, yes. In Tyre, in Ancient Greece, they chained the god Apollo to an altar, to secure protection for their city. Stop him getting away and limit his power. In Rome, they only unbound Saturn once a year, for a great festival of chaos, because it was too dangerous to leave him free and unfettered all the time.'

'Um. Right.'

'In Modern Europe it tends less to be gods, though, and more demons and witches and the like. Same thing, arguably, but imprisoned in bottles and . . . needles, I think? Though I'm not sure of the logic of that one. There's a witch in a bottle in the Ashmolean Museum. Or is it the Pitt Rivers . . . ?' She trailed off.

'Putting a chain on a statue seems different to putting a witch in a bottle,' said Summer, struggling to keep up.

'Well, it's about containment, isn't it? I think that's the idea, anthropologically speaking . . . But yes, you're right. European legends tend to be more about imprisoning an evil force. As I understand it, there were spirits who, once they were burned or drowned or what have you . . . came back.

So they had to be caught. In bottles. That's what people believed, anyway.'

A little shiver went through Summer.

'Evil?'

'Well, yes. Devils and so forth.'

'Witches.'

'Indeed.'

'Thanks,' said Summer and went back to her book – but she couldn't concentrate now on what she was reading. The words floated, like leaves on a pond. She thought about a witch springing forth from a bottle, decanting into dark, solid reality, boots included, and followed by a cat. She thought about being burned, or drowned, and how that might feel.

On the way out of the library, she paused at the desk. Mrs Brathwaite was doing a crossword in *The Times* that seemed to require a lot of sucking of pens. All her pens had chewed ends. She kept them in a pot.

'Er, Mrs Brathwaite?'

'Val.'

'Uh-huh. What . . . what would you do if you found a bottle? With a witch in it?' Summer took all inflection out of her voice, made it as flat as a road.

Mrs Brathwaite smiled. It flicked a switch in her face, making it shine. 'Well,' she said, 'I'd take it to a museum, I suppose.'

'Yeah.'

Mrs Brathwaite smiled wider. She quickly wrote down a crossword answer that had seemingly just come to her.

'What I would never, ever do, of course,' she said, 'is open it.'

Chapter 8

Summer turned the corner into her street, and there was the witch.

The lights of the house were on, the windows dark gold against the blue-black night, where the other houses were whiter. Mr Pattinson said it was the old single-paned glass. When you were inside, you could see the warp of it, the almost liquid way it slightly curved.

The witch was standing away from the street lights so that anyone looking out wouldn't see her. The silhouette of her erect, thin body and her hat formed a dark cut-out from the rest of the street, as if some tailor of light had snipped her out of reality.

'Did you think of the magic you want from me?' she asked, as Summer came near.

'I don't want any magic,' said Summer. She was thinking

of what Mrs Brathwaite had said about evil forces.

She stared at the witch. Did she look evil?

Yes, Summer answered herself. *Yes, she did.*

'Everyone wants magic,' said the witch, with a small, unfathomable smile.

Summer thought about the bottle: *What I would never, ever do, of course, is open it.*

'Not me,' she said.

The witch smiled again. It wasn't like Mrs Brathwaite – it didn't illuminate her features. Just rearranged them.

'Very well. Go in, then, to your mother and father. To the tedium of your life. Be grateful you let me out of the bottle: I will spare you when I wreak my vengeance.'

She turned and began to walk away. The cat, Tobias, was suddenly at her feet, as if conjured from the ground.

'Vengeance?' said Summer.

'On the town.'

'Oh.'

Summer started towards the house. She didn't like the idea of vengeance. There were people in the town she felt fondly towards. Not many, admittedly. But Aishwarya. Mrs Brathwaite. Her elderly tea companions: Mrs Cardle down the street, and Mr Rowntree up the hill.

She paused, turned around and walked back a few paces. 'They're not *my* mother and father,' she said. The words didn't seem to have come from her head, just from her mouth.

'No? But this –' the witch winced as she pointed to it – 'is your house, yes?'

'Sort of. The people who own it . . . they're my foster parents.'

'Foster parents?'

'They sort of . . . adopted me. But not really.'

'Ah! You're a foundling. Like me. Your mother abandoned you on a doorstep?'

'Er, no. She – she – she couldn't look after me. An agency took me away from her and put me in . . . different houses.'

A dark look passed over the witch's face. 'An agency? The parish?'

'Um. Social services. So . . . a bit like that.'

'You're less of a foundling, then, than a takenling. One who was taken.'

'Er . . .'

'Inelegant phrasing. I apologize. My tongue runs away from me sometimes. It got me drowned once.'

It was weird to hear someone talk casually about their own death. 'You were a . . . foundling?' said Summer.

In the eyes of the witch was rain, falling, and clouds, dark clouds, boiling. And then there wasn't.

'Left on a step,' she said. 'To die in the snow. The parish took me in.'

'I'm sorry,' said Summer.

'It was a long time ago,' said the witch. She looked up at the old house, with its golden light. 'Later, though, there was a woman who to me was like a mother,' she continued. 'She lived in this house that you live in now, as did I.'

Summer turned, startled, to look at the place where she lived. She thought of the dragon underneath, and how old it was. She wondered if the Pattinsons knew their house had been the home of a witch.

'*You* lived here?' she said.

'Yes,' said the witch. 'With a good woman. She taught me poultices, and the use of herbs. But then they came for her with pitchforks and scythes.'

'What, really?'

Summer looked around, at the brick-and-concrete buildings of the street, at the lights and the road markings.

'This was mostly farmland, then,' said the witch.

'Still. Pitchforks. It just sounds a bit . . . quaint.'

'Have you seen a pitchfork? Or a scythe?'

'No.'

'They're not quaint. They are big and sharp.'

Summer nodded. 'I see,' she said.

The witch rubbed at her forehead and narrowed her eyes. 'You live in a house that is not your house, and you are motherless. And there is no magic you would ask of me?'

Now there was a glowing light in her eyes, like the gleam of light on a blade.

'I . . .'

'Think of your wildest dreams. Think of the things you wish for. I can grant you those wishes. I have power in great abundance.'

Summer looked at the door to the house. It was possible – she thought – that it had been open all along, yesterday. That it had never been locked.

'*Do* you?' she said. 'Have power? Real power, I mean?'

'Oh yes,' said the witch.

'So you could turn me into a frog, or whatever?'

The witch angled her head. 'I could. But why would you want to be a frog?'

'I don't, really.'

'Then it would be a peculiar thing to turn you into one.'

The witch closed her eyes and her head moved, in small increments, as if she were looking at something in the darkness behind her eyelids.

'My magic is a reservoir, not a stream, and it is not full,' she said.

'Right,' said Summer, in a somewhat sarcastic tone. 'So you don't have power?'

'I didn't say that,' said the witch. 'I have enough. Here. Take my hand.' She thrust it out.

Summer looked at it. 'I don't . . . I don't really like to do that any more,' she said.

'Why not?'

'Viruses.'

The witch looked blank.

'Diseases.'

Now the witch narrowed her eyes. 'I was in a bottle. I'm not precisely alive. I don't carry diseases.' Her hand was still held out.

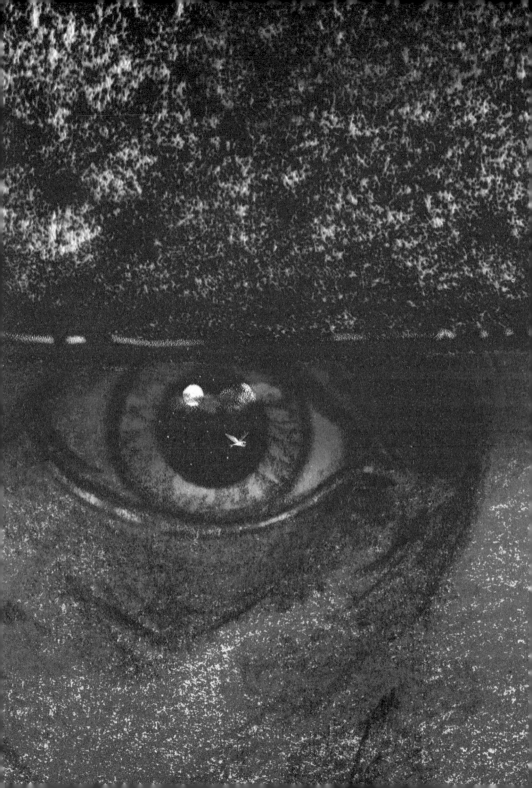

Summer sighed and, feeling a little trepidation, put out her hand. The witch's fingers were cold and smooth, like stone. Summer felt a tremor that shivered up her wrist and down her arm, and then hummed in her chest, like a tune. All her hairs stood on end: actually stood up, wavering palely on her forearms like weeds underwater, as if she were close to a source of static electricity. And something under her skin began to move, to shift.

'What . . .' she began.

The front garden blurred, contracting. Summer's skin was suddenly wavy and iridescent and soft. Her arms pushed down, lofting her into the air, and she rushed up into the sky, past the windows, past the roof of the house.

The creature beside her was a bird with the eyes of the witch, and Summer spoke with a whistle, a chirp, and she understood that she was a bird, too.

Chapter 9

Soaring above the houses,
over the rooftops, the
witch spoke to Summer
with a liquid song that
meant *I am starling*.

The sun was setting,
and the sky was the
purple-blue of late
winter at dusk, a single
star or planet gleaming
above the roofs of
the houses, the trees
bare and black
against the glow.

Other starlings were suddenly around them, a small

flock of them, and Summer's wings adjusted without her telling them to, her tail, too. She was banking, then flying alongside one of them, another on her other wing. They spiralled, looping round an old oak tree at the end of the road, and then off towards the river.

She opened her mouth, and song spilled out.

The starlings swirled in the sky, looking for insects, and Summer swooped with them, the witch beside her. The air was all around her and in her, under her feathers – she was a thing of the sky. She didn't think she had ever felt such joy; and then she didn't think at all.

She just flew, and turned, and dived and soared. There

was still an inky brightness in the sky, and the starlings around her were dark points in it against the paling sunlight – something like the opposite of sparks – as they whirled upwards.

Then the witch flew closer, and music came from her throat, and the music said it was time to land.

Summer lowered her beak towards the roofs and the cars, the air whistling past her flat ears; the ground coming towards her like a map zooming in. It occurred to her that she didn't know how to land, and that there might be someone on the street to see, but then her wings were out and flat and the air was hard against them. In seconds, she was on her feet on the stones of the front garden.

Feathers retracted into skin.

Tail became backbone.

The garden and house shrank downwards as Summer grew up, until she was standing there, the witch in front of her. Tobias was licking his fur, looking superior and bored.

'I always liked being a bird,' said the witch.

'*Chiiiiirp*,' said Summer.

'Ah. Sometimes it takes a little while,' said the witch.

Summer swallowed. She hadn't realized how little she

could see, as a human – how lacking in detail her vision was. All the scent had now gone from the air, the flowers, and the worms working under the earth. But it was nice to feel the gravel beneath her shoes. 'All right,' she said, slowly. 'So you do have some power.'

The witch smiled. 'Three things,' she said. 'Ask me for three things today, tomorrow and the day after that. And I will make them true. There is a magic in threes.'

'And then?'

'And then I will leave you.'

'You have to leave the town, too,' said Summer. 'There are nice people here.'

'Are there? When you were walking home, I heard a child say terrible things to you and the girl you walked with.'

Summer swallowed hard at the idea that the witch had been there, somehow, listening.

'Three things. Then you leave the town alone,' said Summer.

'Is not leaving the town alone a wish, in itself?'

'No,' said Summer, forcing more confidence into her voice than she felt. 'It's a condition.'

The witch smiled that smile again, that recalibration of

her face. 'It is a compact,' she said. 'Between you and I.'

Summer figured that meant it was a deal.

She thought about the things she had never had. There was one thing she wanted, of course, but it was so big, she almost couldn't think it. So small, too. *Just three words*. But she tried to think of other things that were missing, other holes inside herself.

She thought of the kids, throwing stones.

She thought of the people in her class who were like flowers, everyone blasting beams of niceness towards them, soaking up sunlight, all day long. What it must be, to be a petal like Aishwarya, rather than a weed.

'I just . . .' she said. 'I just want everyone to like me.'

'That can be done,' said the witch. She took Summer's arm, linked her own with it. Her body wasn't cold, but it was entirely without heat. Like wood. 'Yet I hunger for tea. Sweetmeats. Pastry. Cake. To work magic on an empty stomach is a hard thing. And this house of yours, which is also not yours, is somewhere I cannot enter.'

Summer wasn't exactly sure what sweetmeats were, but she knew who would have biscuits. 'We could try Mr Rowntree's house,' she said. 'He's usually there at this time.'

'Will you be missed? In there?'

The witch didn't even look at the old house this time. She said *there* like it was a dirty word.

'Oh no. They barely notice if I'm home or not,' said Summer. But she said it with an uncomfortable squirm in her tummy. She wasn't totally sure it was true.

'Terrible,' said the witch. 'But also perfect. To Mr Rowntree's we go, then! And no dilly-dallying.'

She headed off down the street, pulling Summer along with her, and if Summer wondered at the fact that she knew which way to go, it was only much later.

Chapter 10

The quickest way to Mr Rowntree's was up the high street, but Summer thought it might attract attention if she walked there with a woman dressed in olden-days clothes. Instead, she cut through the hotel car park, past the back of the supermarket, and then up the little alleyway by the hotel entrance to Sheep Street. They crossed the road, and she led the way to an alley – a tiny, thin canyon between old houses, medieval windows leaning into the space.

She entered the narrow alley – then sensed she was alone.

Summer turned round and saw the witch still standing on Sheep Street, a strange expression on her face.

'It's this way?' Summer said, indicating the alley.

The witch looked up. 'No. I will not go through there.'

Tobias stood next to her. Every hair on his body, it seemed, was standing vertical. His tail was up, like an exclamation mark. He was hissing. Summer had never seen a cat look like that.

Summer glanced around. The sun was setting, the low light firing the old windows of the alley with flame. But there was no one around. Nothing threatening.

St Mary Lane

said the little old sign set into the wall next to her.

'It's just at the end,' said Summer. 'Otherwise we have to go all the way around.'

'Then we shall have to go all the way around,' said the witch. Not moving.

Summer sighed. 'Okay.'

She turned back, and they had to walk past the coppiced trees on Sheep Street to Tanner's Lane, up to the rec, then down again. A ridiculous route, but the witch's body had relaxed a little, the tension and stiffness gone out of it. As they passed the little gate to the rec, a dog leaped towards them, barking at Tobias, who sniffed haughtily.

The witch made a small circular movement with her hand, and the dog stood still, confused.

They walked on. As they approached Mr Rowntree's house, Summer paused, suddenly feeling strange and uneasy. It was like taking a vampire round for tea on a sunny day. She pushed the feeling down, deep inside herself, and put a lid on it so it couldn't get out. Made herself into a bottle, with smooth, hard sides.

'We might want to leave Tobias behind,' she said. 'Cats don't normally follow people around like dogs. It looks weird.'

'*Charmed*,' said Tobias, who promptly disappeared, quick as a candle flame going out.

At Mr Rowntree's door, Summer knocked, and when he answered the little old man widened his eyes at the witch. This made them go very large indeed, as they were already magnified by his big glasses. He reached up a hand and turned on his hearing aid. Then he looked at the witch with frank interest.

'Friend of yours?' he said to Summer.

'You can call me Sarah,' said the witch, holding out her hand to him.

Summer was struck by two things: that she hadn't even

thought to ask the witch's name. And that the witch hadn't precisely said Sarah *was* her name.

'Bill,' said Mr Rowntree, shaking hands with the witch.

Apparently, it was Summer's day for learning people's names. She'd always known him as Mr Rowntree. They'd first met at the library, where he'd been a volunteer for a while, working alongside Mrs Brathwaite. Then they'd chatted over his fence when she was hanging out at the swings in the rec after school, mindlessly swinging and swinging. Gradually as they'd got to know each other, she'd ended up going in for tea. It wasn't like she was in the habit of just waltzing into strangers' houses.

'My, er, friend is hungry,' said Summer. 'She sort of, well, doesn't have a house to go to at the moment.' As she said it, she realized she wasn't exactly lying.

'Ah! Another stray.' He looked the witch up and down. 'My speciality, it would appear.' He smiled at Summer. 'Well, Summer, after you.'

Summer went into the hall, Mr Rowntree behind her, and it took them a moment to realize the witch wasn't behind them. She was still standing at the doorway, looking somehow both expectant and hesitant. Bill turned and looked curious for a moment, and then his expression cleared, like clouds from a sky.

'Sorry!' he said. 'Do come in.' He made a welcoming gesture towards the inside of the house.

The witch smiled and stepped over the threshold. Summer shivered a little at that. At the way she could only go in once invited.

Bill led the way towards the living room. 'Have a seat,' he said. 'I'll fetch tea. I made marmalade.'

'Marmalade!' said the witch. Said *Sarah*. 'Delicious!' She smiled as he left the room.

She and Summer were sitting on the kind of soft, voluminous sofas that only older people seemed to own. The TV was on in the corner, but quietly, with subtitles on.

'You're really hungry?' said Summer. 'Even though you're –' she dropped her voice – 'a ghost?'

'I'm not a ghost. I'm dead. And yes. I may perish from hunger. I would if I had not already perished some three hundred—'

'Shush!' said Summer, as Mr Rowntree came back, bearing a tray.

He set it down on the glass coffee table and poured tea

into three cups, with saucers, from a large teapot. Then
he put a plate of buttered toast with marmalade on to the
middle of the table, as well as a pot of sugar with a spoon in
it and a jug of milk. He handed round the cups.

'How marvellous!' said the witch, whom Summer
struggled to think of as Sarah, even if that wasn't her name.
'Do you mind terribly if I help myself to sugar? I do like to
sweeten my tea.'

'Of course,' said Mr Rowntree. Summer refused to think
of him as Bill.

'Of course you mind or of course you don't . . . ?'

Mr Rowntree liked sudoku and puzzles, and watching
quiz shows. He smiled at this. 'I don't mind.'

'And the toast – may I take a slice . . . ?'

Summer hadn't heard the witch speaking like this before.

'Make yourself at home,' said Mr Rowntree.

The witch smiled back at that: the mechanics of a mouth
lifting up at the edges. 'Thank you,' she said, and a breeze
lifted in the room, from some open window. The lamp
hanging above them swung slightly, and the tassels dangling
from the runner on the sideboard stirred.

'You're welcome,' said Bill. 'What were we . . .' He

scratched his eyebrow. He looked pale all of a sudden, and Summer saw his hand twitch.

'We were just about to have tea,' said the witch, gently.

'Ah yes!' He took a slice of toast and ate it, delicately. Then he sipped his tea.

'It's very kind of you,' said Summer. 'I know I come round a lot; it's just I don't have many places to—'

'It's just that you're my friend,' said Mr Rowntree, firmly. 'And one helps friends.' He looked at the witch. 'Speaking of which, do you need anything? Clothes? That sort of thing?'

Summer was confused until she remembered she'd basically said the witch was homeless.

The witch looked down at herself. 'Oh no, I'm perfectly happy with my poor garb,' she said. 'It has served me well these many years.'

'Righto. Well, let me know if I—'

'In fact,' interrupted the witch, 'I am most happy to have met you, and to have had tea, which was a great pleasure and something I have not partaken of in some time, but Summer and I must be going.'

'Must we?' said Summer.

She wasn't even sure the witch had eaten anything, despite

saying she was hungry. Though she had lifted the teacup to her lips. Now she set it down, seemingly full.

'Oh yes,' said the witch, standing. She looked out at the darkening sky. 'It's the magic hour, you see.'

Soon they were outside again, standing by the rec, and Tobias melted out of the air and into the witch's arms.

'I feel better for that,' said the witch. 'Now. A spell for everyone to like you.' She touched Summer's forehead and muttered briefly.

Then she stepped back.

'Is that it?' said Summer.

But she wasn't talking to anything. She was talking to the cooling air, and the dark sky, and the crows wheeling against black branches overhead. The witch was gone.

Tobias yowled as he fell, twisting, and landed on his paws.

'I wish she wouldn't do that,' he said.

Chapter 11

Time passed like the space between chapters in a book, and it was somehow registration at school the next morning. Summer didn't have any particular memory of what had happened when she got home the night before.

'Summer Scrivens,' said Miss Austin.

Summer wasn't Summer's *real* name, but it was her middle name, and she couldn't remember a time when people hadn't called her by it.

'Present,' said Summer.

'*Yeah* she is,' said Devlin, one of the coolest and hardest kids in Year Six. He didn't sound as if he was being ironic.

Marc, who was on the football team, turned to Summer and raised his fist – and she flinched, before realizing he wanted to fist-bump her. She raised her own hand, and he bumped it, then mimed his own hand exploding. 'Summer in the *house*,' he said.

Someone else actually *whooped*.

'I think we're all delighted Summer is here,' said Miss Austin, with a slight roll of her eyes. But a smile, too.

Summer thought: *This is weird.*

Then, in class, she was going to sit at the back as usual, but Ruby made a place for her at the front with the other Year Six girls and beckoned her over. Summer wasn't even *in* Year Six. It was a very small school, and they had Year Five and Year Six together. But she joined them, anyway. She noticed Aishwarya staring at her as she went, from her own little table of Year Five top-girls.

Summer sat down. Wordlessly, Ruby showed her the tie-dye bracelet on her wrist, and motioned for the other girls to show theirs. Then she handed one to Summer.

'Put it on,' she said. 'Welcome to the gang.'

Nor did the weirdness stop there.

When it came time to read their homework, which was an application to spy school, Mrs Taylor got Summer to read hers out, and then praised it lavishly and at some length. This was *highly* unusual – mostly, Summer spent her days being told off, or sighed sadly at, as if she was a problem to be solved. In fairness, that was because Summer sometimes didn't do her homework; when it wasn't fun things like writing, anyway. She liked stories.

Then, instead of flicking stuff at her or pretending to blow their brains out with pistols made of their fingers, the other kids nodded, seriously.

I could get used to this, thought Summer.

At lunch, they went out on the paddock – which was a big bit of grass that the parent group had raised money to buy from the farm next door, and Summer started towards the obstacle course everyone usually played on, even the unpopular ones, because the teachers were watching, and everyone had to share.

But Ruby made a gesture at her again – waved her over to the *shed*. The shed was where the sports equipment was stored, and where the popular girls hung out, and *only* the popular girls. The teachers turned a blind eye because the popular girls were also supposed to be in charge of organizing and tidying up the shed, so that they would learn some responsibility. It was their own little castle where no one else was allowed.

Until now.

Summer hesitated for a moment. But then a flock of starlings caught her eye, whirling round a tree at the back of the paddock before landing on the wooden turrets and roofs of the obstacle course. Dozens of them. Some of the kids looked up at them and pointed. Summer felt that they were looking at her, focused on her, their beady eyes swivelled towards her.

She's here, said a voice in her mind. Her own voice. Her original accent, which she never used. The voice she'd got from her mother, the voice that belonged to her own, true name.

Summer turned to the shed again. She didn't want to look at the starlings. Took a deep breath. Then walked past Aishwarya, who was pretty much open-mouthed at this point, and into the shed. Scarlett was sitting on some crash mats, picking at her nails. She smiled at Summer. Poppy was throwing a tennis ball and catching it on the back of her hand. She also smiled at Summer.

And Ruby, leaning against a stack of cones, smiled the widest.

'So, Summer,' she said, 'what's it like being a foster kid? It must be so cool.'

'C-cool?' said Summer.

'Yeah. Like, no parents to hassle you and stuff.'

Summer wasn't sure how to answer this.

'Oh,' she said, 'it's one endless party, you know? The other day, my foster brothers ate so much ice cream that one of them was sick, and I ended up helping my foster mum clean it up. I didn't even get any ice cream. Though it was pistachio, on the plus side. I don't like pistachio.' She paused. 'Well, I *did* like pistachio until I had to clean it up as sick.'

Ruby and the others laughed, uproariously.

'You're funny!' said Scarlett. Without a trace of sarcasm.

'Er, thanks,' said Summer.

After that, they talked about all kinds of things. Ruby's boyfriend, Sam, mostly. Summer thought the idea of Ruby and Sam being girlfriend and boyfriend was kind of silly, really – they just held hands sometimes and hardly ever spoke to each other – but she didn't say so. They talked about bands Summer hadn't heard of, and ponies – Ruby was very into ponies – and whose parents had signed the forms for the summer trip and whether Sam might agree to a slow dance at the disco at the end of term.

They talked about Mrs Myer and what a pain she was – *a pain in the bum* was how Poppy put it, and so Summer hung her voice on to the hook in her mind she had for the high-pitched head teacher and spoke:

'*Tuck in your shirts, boys,*' she said. '*I want to see every shirt tucked in!*'

Scarlett almost fell off her stool laughing, and Poppy snorted strawberry milk out of her nose. 'Do me!' she said. 'Do me!'

And Summer did, and not even that kindly – she used Poppy's voice to say that she was hoping Weird Kevin who bred guinea pigs would invite her to the Year Six ball later that year – and they all laughed, anyway, and fist-bumped her.

Summer did think, at one point, that it might be more fun to be outside on the slide. But she was in the shed, with the cool girls! And on the obstacle course, of course, were starlings. Dozens and dozens of them. Or had she imagined that? Their wings and claws and beaks. So much of birds was made of hard material – their feathers tipped with sharp, hollow points, their mouths like nutcrackers.

She pushed that thought to the back of her mind and tried to enjoy her weird new lunchbreak.

Not that the weirdness stopped. All afternoon, Mrs Taylor smiled at her, which helped. And it was true, it was what Summer had hoped: it was like she was a flower now, soaking up the sun, instead of a little ragged weed, growing in a crack.

After school, they went out of the gates together, she and the Year Six girls. They passed Aishwarya, whose eyes narrowed as Summer walked by her.

She paused. 'Um. Aishwarya can walk with us, right?'

Ruby tutted. 'She's a Year *Five*.'

'So am I,' said Summer.

'Yes. But you're cool. Isn't she, girls?'

'Yes,' chorused the other girls, and they all linked arms, Summer, too. Summer in the middle.

She felt bad – and she did turn back to glance at Aishwarya, who was looking away – but she also loved it.

Chapter 12

Summer and the other girls sailed out of school together and walked as far as they could in a chain, until they had to start splitting off for their own roads.

Eventually, Summer was left on her own, outside the house where she lived. The house with the hole in it. The house with the dragon in it. Then Tobias was suddenly round her feet, sinuous.

'Good day at school?' he purred.

'Yes,' said Summer. 'A bit weird, actually. But yes.' She paused.

'I'm glad,' said the witch, appearing from nothing, and Summer startled a little, nudging Tobias with her foot.

'Hey,' he said.

'Sorry,' said Summer.

Tobias curled up in a patch of sunshine and began licking

himself. 'Clumsiness does not suit a girl,' he said.

'At least I'm not cleaning my bum with my tongue,' said Summer. 'And what's it got to do with girls, anyway?'

Tobias didn't say anything to that.

Sarah, the witch, was peering at Summer. 'It was good, then, the spell?'

'Yes,' said Summer. 'It was great. Um. Thank you.'

It was also, she knew, wrong. It was wrong, and she shouldn't be doing it, but somehow she couldn't stop. To be popular by trickery. To exclude others, like Aishwarya. Wrong but in some strange way thrilling. She wondered if this was how the bullies had felt, as they threw stones at her. Yet this was another thought she pushed down, wriggling, struggling.

'You're welcome,' said the witch. 'Sometimes all people need is a little push.'

Summer considered that. 'I guess,' she said.

'So. You have had your first spell,' the witch said. 'What about the second?'

Summer had a sudden flashback to Aishwarya, her eyebrows drawing together as Summer walked past, but she flicked it away to a corner of her mind. She looked down at herself. She was wearing the school uniform Mrs Pattinson had chosen for her. White shirt, grey trousers. Girls were allowed to wear trousers, as an option. Summer hadn't had a school skirt since being in this house. She was grateful to have new things, not hand-me-downs, but she wanted clothes she'd chosen herself, she wanted a bike, even though no one had ever taught her to ride one, and most of all she wanted a phone. So she could text people, be included, talk to Aishwarya – or Ruby and the other girls now, too, she guessed.

Keep up with things. Be on the inside for once, not the outside.

'Money,' she said, a foot in her mind firmly on the head of the thought that was trying to rise up, that was trying to recall to her the metal gleam in the witch's eyes, pushing it back down into the dark. 'I'd like to have lots of money.'

The witch closed her eyes, and stuck out her tongue a bit, as if tasting the air. 'Interesting,' she said. 'Money is more of an idea now, is it, than a thing?'

Summer thought about what she knew about money. Mortgages, loans, credit cards, the stock market. 'I suppose so,' she said.

'Complicated,' said the witch. 'And hard work for a thirsty soul.'

Summer thought of the girls being nice to her, the delicious feeling of it. Imagine having money, too. She didn't care if this was wrong. It was fun.

'Tea at Mr Rowntree's again?' she said a little hesitantly. She was hoping the witch would say no.

'Oh, I think not,' said the witch. 'We'd be imposing, to go two days in a row. Is there anywhere else?'

Summer considered this with a sense of relief. There were cafes, of course, but that wasn't straightforward as an option, with a witch in tow. Who knew what she might say? There was the library, but something made Summer think that putting the witch and the librarian together wasn't a good idea. Something she should have listened to, she realized later.

The only other option was . . .

'Mrs Cardle,' she said. 'She's always baking.'

'Wonderful!' said the witch. 'Lead the way!'

Summer did, and her stomach churned with excitement – and fear.

Chapter 13

Mrs Cardle was walking with her stick down the road towards her door when they came round the corner. She had kept up her mobility since her hip operation.

'Summer!' she said, smiling. 'I made it to the postbox by the crematorium today. Saw a buzzard, and the crocuses are coming out.'

'Ah, you're getting further every day,' said Summer. 'You'll be in Tarlington by summer.'

'I hope so,' said Mrs Cardle. 'Good pub in Tarlington. And there are often muntjacs and hares by the single-lane road.'

'Right,' said Summer, who had never seen a muntjac or a hare, and wouldn't know what to do if she did, or what they might look like, or why it would matter. A hare looked a bit like a rabbit, she thought? But Mrs Cardle loved that stuff.

'Oh, what I wouldn't do for a bit of hare stew,' said the witch. 'I haven't had it for such a long time.'

Mrs Cardle gave her a slightly confused smile and put out her hand, to shake the witch's. 'It's been decades since I've had hare stew,' she said. 'Not since the war, I don't think.'

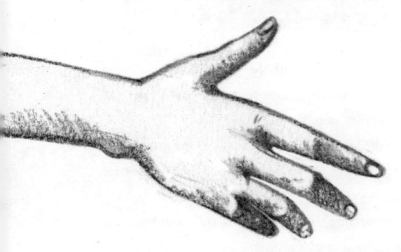

'Her father was a gamekeeper,' said Summer, quickly.

'Ah!' said Mrs Cardle, turning back to the witch. 'So . . . you must be a relative of Summer's . . . ?' she said, a little hopefully. 'I'm Mrs Cardle.'

'An aunt,' said the witch. 'Distant. I was . . . away, and now I'm back. My name is Sarah.' She shook Mrs Cardle's outstretched hand.

'I see. Terrible shame about the girl's mother.'

'Indeed,' said the witch.

'I do try to feed her up as best I can!' said Mrs Cardle, in that false-bright voice that grown-ups did when talking about sad things. 'Cake after school. She does her homework

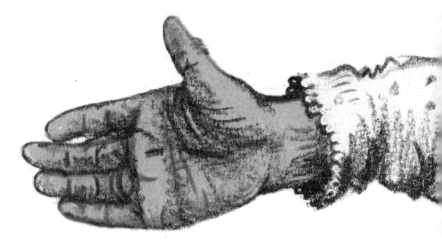

too, mind, most times. And reads. I have lots of books.'

'That's lovely,' said the witch. 'She's very lucky to have you.'

Summer's heart twisted. *Was* she?

Mrs Cardle lit like a lantern though; glowed from the eyes. 'Thank you. And are you . . . that is . . . is the fostering arrangement . . . going to continue?'

'I very much hope not,' said the witch, and winked at Summer.

Mrs Cardle nodded, as if that was good news, and to be hoped for. Which, Summer supposed, it was. The sprightly old woman opened her front door and waved them in. Sarah the witch hesitated at the doorway.

'Come in, come in, do,' said Mrs Cardle. 'I have Battenberg left over.'

The witch bowed and entered behind Summer. Summer hesitated, thinking of how the witch had not gone into Mr Rowntree's house until invited, feeling uncomfortable and itchy on the inside of her skin, though she wasn't sure why.

Within the house it was all homely clutter and warmth, with cushions on every available surface. Summer and the witch sat, while Mrs Cardle busied herself making tea and putting out slices of the cake, with its neat squares of yellow and red, on flowery china plates.

'So, will you be looking into adoption?' said Mrs Cardle. 'I had no idea Summer had . . . anyone. In terms of family, that is.'

Summer felt the sympathy in those words and a little twist in her belly.

'I imagine so,' said the witch. 'I've only just arrived. There's a lot for me to do.'

Something about the way she was lying so smoothly, had so quickly worked out what Mrs Cardle wanted to hear, felt to Summer like a cold draught on her arms.

'I'm sure,' said Mrs Cardle. 'Starting with cake! Do help yourself.'

'Thank you,' said the witch.

She took a plate and a cup of tea, which she sipped. Or seemed to sip. The level of the tea did not go down, Summer noticed. The witch put the cup on the table again. 'I'm terribly sorry,' she said. 'You wouldn't happen to have a privy I could use?'

'A privy! Well, I have a downstairs loo. It's just down the hall on the right.'

'Thank you. I appreciate it.'

Mrs Cardle waved this away. '*Mi casa es su casa,*' she said.

'I'm sorry?'

'Oh, it's Spanish,' said Mrs Cardle. 'My husband and I retired to the Costa Brava, but when he died I came home. I missed the English flowers, anyway, and the hedgerows.

It means something like . . . *be my guest*. Or *make yourself at home.*'

The witch smiled that smile again, the one that didn't involve anything but muscle, and nerve, and sinew. 'You're too kind,' she said.

On the table, the teacups rattled a little in their saucers, and Summer looked up, to see if a window was open. Metallic shiver of a teaspoon against a rim. Mrs Cardle blinked, and slumped for a moment in her chair, before seeming to collect herself.

The witch disappeared round the door.

'Ooh,' said Mrs Cardle. 'I had a bit of a funny turn there. Felt like someone walked over my grave.'

Summer felt the skin on her arms tighten. She hugged herself, quickly, though the house was not cold.

'Have some Battenberg, dear, do,' said Mrs Cardle. A little colour was coming back into her cheeks.

Summer duly ate some cake and took a sip of tea. 'It's delicious,' she said. She couldn't taste anything at all. 'Thanks, Mrs Cardle.'

'You're welcome, my girl. Now.' She spoke a bit more quietly and leaned in, a smile on her face.

'This aunt. Must be exciting?'

'It's . . . yes. It is.'

Summer smiled back, feeling the icy, uncertain fear inside her melting. It *was* exciting, though of course not for the reason Mrs Cardle thought. Magic and secrets and power. The power to make people like her. To get money. And then to ask for . . . something else. Something bigger. Something she couldn't quite make into a full thought yet, in case that made it vanish, like the looping trail of a sparkler in darkness.

'Well, I'm happy for you,' said Mrs Cardle, squeezing Summer's knee. ''Bout time you had a bit of love in your life.'

Summer blinked at that, her eyes unexpectedly watery, her vision blurred. 'Er, thanks,' she said.

The witch came back in, and they made small talk for a while, until Mrs Cardle suddenly put a finger in the air.

'I have something for you!' she said. 'A present.'

'But we've only just met,' the witch said.

'Oh, I mean for—'

'I know,' said the witch. 'It was a jest.' Her eyes gleamed.

'Ah!' said Mrs Cardle, laughing, and Summer laughed, too.

She had a witch in her life who made things happen for

her and made jokes. Things were looking up. She didn't know why she'd been uncomfortable just now.

Mrs Cardle went to the sideboard and brought over an oblong gift-wrapped object, which she gave to Summer. 'From Mrs Brathwaite at the library,' she said. 'She stopped me on the street and asked me to pass it on to you.'

'Er, thanks,' said Summer. It wasn't her birthday for ages. She looked at the two older women and felt self-conscious. 'I'll open it later.'

'Speaking of later, and getting later, we should be going,' said the witch, standing up. 'Thank you *so* much for tea.'

'Oh. Oh right, yes. Well, it was lovely to meet you,' said Mrs Cardle.

As quickly as they'd entered the house, the witch ushered them out, bundling Summer ahead of her, and soon they were back on the street, a chill breeze blowing. It was only just gone four o'clock. Summer held the present under her coat. Spells, friends and now a gift – which she hadn't even wished for. She was having quite the week. But still, she couldn't totally abandon the people she'd relied on up till now.

'In a hurry?' she asked the witch, a little sharply. 'I hope we didn't offend Mrs Cardle by leaving so—'

Sarah, the witch, clicked her fingers softly and handed something to Summer. A small piece of paper. On it was written her name, the name of the bank on the high street, a bank account number and a sort code.

'What's this?' said Summer.

'A very large amount of money,' said the witch. 'If you hurry, you may make it to the bank before it closes.' She paused and reached into the air as if it had a pocket in it. She drew out a thin plastic card. 'One, two, three, four,' she said.

Then, in a blink, she was gone.

Chapter 14

That evening, Summer was helping to make puzzles in the den when Mrs Pattinson called out in shock from the living room. What the Original Children liked to do was to make all the jigsaw puzzles – they had a pile of them in the cupboard – into a kind of tiled and tessellated carpet covering the whole floor, dinosaurs and pigs and jungles and underwater scenes abutting each other and stretching from wall to wall. A couple of the pieces were missing, but had been for years, apparently. Summer imagined them – the toe of a T-Rex, a monkey's tail – far under the sofa or beneath the bookshelves, gathering dust.

'What is it?' called Mr Pattinson from the kitchen.

'Come and look,' said Mrs Pattinson, still in the living room.

Oscar and Ethan were on their feet in moments, which is what happens if you say within the hearing of small children that there is something to look at. They hurried into the living room, and Summer followed.

Mr Pattinson was standing next to his wife, rubbing absently at his jaw. The overhead light was on, the big light as Mrs Pattinson called it – she preferred the lamps generally – and was casting long shadows from Summer's foster parents on to the furniture.

'You see what I mean?' said Mrs Pattinson.

'Hmm,' her husband said. He didn't sound happy.

Summer and the boys went to stand next to them.

Summer blinked.

The hole was – very clearly – bigger.

Before, it had stretched about two metres across the living room. Now it was . . . three metres maybe? Considerably larger, anyway. The floorboards had split and warped around its edges, like a cannon hole in a ship, and a couple of the poles holding up the barrier tape had fallen in, dangling by their own tape, but the hole itself didn't look fundamentally different – its walls were still rock that sloped down into darkness below.

'This won't help with the insurance claim,' said Mr Pattinson, with a sigh.

Mrs Pattinson patted his arm. 'I'm sure there'll be a solution, darling,' she said.

'Can't they just fill it with concrete?' said Oscar.

'Apparently not,' said Mr Pattinson. 'They, um, think there's some kind of cave down there.'

Summer felt her skin tingle, picturing the dragon deep down below. Slumbering. Or doing whatever it was dragons did when there was no one around. Summer tried not to think about it too much, but when she did she hoped that the dragon's role had been to introduce her to the witch – and that there would be no other reason to see him again.

'But what if it keeps getting bigger?' said Ethan. 'What if it grows and grows and eats up the whole house?'

'That's not going to happen,' said Mrs Pattinson, but she didn't sound totally convinced.

'Nothing's eating the house,' said Mr Pattinson. 'It's eating our money, which is a different thing.'

'What?' said Ethan.

'Nothing,' said Mr Pattinson. 'Never mind.'

Summer touched her pocket, where the bank card was. Money. She had money now. At least she thought she did.

Just for a moment, a thought crossed her mind, like a

cloud blocking out the sun. That it might be her wishes that had made the hole get bigger. Being popular – having money. Or perhaps it was those trips to have tea with her elderly friends. Hadn't something happened there, in those cosy homes? Summer felt sure it had, but also it was nothing she could put her finger on. She wrapped her arms round herself.

Mrs Pattinson, reading this wrong, came and patted her shoulder. 'It's all right, Summer,' she said. 'We'll sort it out.'

Summer wondered about that. She wondered if they *could* sort it out. But when they left the living room, and while she and the boys finished building the puzzles, and all through dinner, she kept that thought locked up, buried; poured concrete over it so it was walled into its cave in her mind, unable to get out.

Chapter 15

Next day, after school, the cashier at the bank looked up at Summer, then back down at the papers he was shuffling on the little table where he sat. There was a thick pane of clear plastic between them. The sun was shining outside, which helped a lot with not thinking about holes in living-room floors getting bigger, and what that might mean.

'You'll have to speak to the manager,' the cashier said. 'I'll buzz you in.'

'Buzz me in . . . ?'

'To her office.'

He picked up a phone and spoke into it softly. Then he indicated a door behind Summer; a dark wooden door with a plaque on it.

'You can go through,' he said.

Summer took her little piece of paper and knocked on the

door, then opened it. The carpet below her feet was thick; her shoes shushed over it.

The manager stood, put out a hand to shake, then seemed to think better of it. She smoothed her skirt. She was middle-aged, with glasses on a cord around her neck, and eyebrows drawn on with make-up.

'Summer?' she said. 'Pleased to, um, meet you. Do sit down.'

Summer sat. 'Is something wrong?' she asked.

'Wrong? Um. No. But . . . do you know how much money is in your bank account?'

Summer shook her head. 'No.'

'It's a little over ten million pounds.'

Summer opened her mouth, then closed it again. In her head, she was reassessing the things she could buy. Not just clothes, not just a phone. A house. A place of her own. Maybe even an island. She was rich. She'd never thought she could be someone rich. And yet here she was.

'I . . . that's a lot,' she said.

'Yes. And of course the account was only opened yesterday. It's more than a little irregular. There are checks we need to undertake. Do you know the source?'

'I'm sorry?'

'Where the money comes from. We have to ask questions. Fraud. You know. And you are a minor. Could we speak to your parents, perhaps?'

'Oh,' said Summer. 'I'm in care. Then I met a woman who said she was my aunt.' This was literally true. 'She opened the account for me.'

'Lucky you,' said the bank manager, not entirely kindly.

Her nametag said Karen McPherson. Summer could smell the coffee on her breath. There was a dying plant on the window sill. Summer thought being a bank manager must be quite a depressing job.

'Can I get some now?' said Summer.

She was thinking of the clothes shop on the high street. The phone store, where they did screen repairs and also sold handsets.

'Some . . . ?'

'Money.'

'Oh gracious, no,' said the woman whose nametag said Karen McPherson. 'I'm going to need a birth certificate, a guardian to countersign, various checks and—'

'But it's mine,' said Summer.

'Not without ID it's not,' said the bank manager, with a degree of satisfaction.

'I can't have anything?'

'Well, if you had a debit card, you could remove two hundred and fifty pounds from a cash machine. But that's our daily limit.'

Summer touched her pocket. *One, two, three, four*, she remembered. She'd assumed the witch was counting down to her disappearance, to her vanishing act, but what if it was . . .

'Couldn't I use the card to buy something?'

'Only if it was activated,' said the manager. 'Which, with such a new account, is unlikely. But you can withdraw money as long as you know the PIN number.'

Summer stood. 'I have to go,' she said.

'Oh well, come back when—'

But Summer was out of the door and round the corner to the cash machine, where she put the card in, meshed gears noisily swallowing it, and tapped in the four numbers when prompted for her PIN.

WOULD YOU LIKE TO SEE YOUR BALANCE?

YES, she tapped.

£10,021,011

She stared. The numbers at the end were her birthday – the 21st of November. The witch knew her birthday. Summer shrugged. The witch, presumably, knew a lot of things.

She tapped on CASH WITHDRAWAL and then had to type in the number because £250 was not a standard option that was offered. There was a brief lull – and the machine began to spit out notes with a slight hiss, depositing them in a little tray. Summer scooped them up and practically ran to the high street to the shops.

Overhead, unseen, starlings swirled round the rooftops, circling the chimneys. Crows lined the tiles and gutters. Red light was in the stone of the buildings, stored all day to be released when the sun went down, and in it the eyes of the birds glittered.

Chapter 16

Summer held the phone in her hand and sighed.

It was an old model, at least three versions behind the latest, but it was all she could afford – and, as the sales assistant Rahim had explained to her at length, it had a decent camera, and it wasn't like anyone really used phones for anything other than surfing the web and social media, anyway.

'Fine, I'll take it,' she said.

'Excellent!' said Rahim, putting the white box in a bag. 'Can I interest you in our insurance plans or—'

'No,' said Summer. 'I can't afford it.'

'Very well, very well,' said Rahim. 'Pleasure doing business with you! As I said, you'll have to come back with a couple of bills addressed to your house to get your mobile number, but you can set up messaging apps using an email address.'

'Right,' said Summer. 'Thank you.'

An email address was one of the few personal things she owned – she had a school one, used for submitting homework and getting news from the office.

As she left, Rahim turned the sign on the door to CLOSED

The street lights were coming on all down the high street. There was a glow over the hill, as if something was on fire, far away.

Summer walked downhill and back home a bit disheartened. In theory, she was a multimillionaire. It was just that, when money was only an idea, as the witch had put it, getting hold of it if you were a foster kid was not a very easy thing to do.

At home, she had to sit through dinner – including grace – before she could get up to her room. Though she found, oddly, that she didn't mind the grace bit so much any more. She *was* grateful for the food, after all. It was roast chicken, and Mr and Mrs Pattinson pulled the wishbone between them, and Mrs Pattinson won the longer end and made a wish when it was all eaten, though she wouldn't say what she wished for. Summer found it kind of amazing: she'd often eaten chicken, but she'd never known a chicken was a thing that could contain a wish.

As she left the kitchen, Mrs Pattinson called her name. She turned. Oscar and Ethan had their heads down, eating their second helpings of pudding.

'Yes?' she said.

'Are you . . . okay?' said Mrs Pattinson.

'Er, yeah. Why?'

Mrs Pattinson frowned. 'You've just not seemed quite yourself lately,' she said.

Summer was surprised by this. She hadn't thought that Mrs Pattinson paid much attention to her.

'Yeah,' said little Ethan, looking up. 'You're like an astronaut, spacewalking. Except at home.'

'Er, sorry,' said Summer. 'Just . . . going through some changes with the girls at school.' This was both true and a huge lie.

'Ah!' said Mr Pattinson, taking a swig of his wine. 'Always a problem with girls. One of the reasons I was always pleased to just have boys!'

Mrs Pattinson cleared her throat. '*Gavin.*'

'What? Oh. Right. Yes. Sorry, Summer. And you, of course.'

'My husband is trying to say—' began Mrs Pattinson, but Summer was already out and heading up the stairs, annoying traitor tears in her eyes.

In her room – which didn't lock, but which Mrs Pattinson had said was 'entirely her own space' – she wiped angrily at her eyes, plugged the phone in and went through the long process of setting it up. Once she'd downloaded the messaging app, she realized she didn't know anyone's number or email address, so she couldn't actually message anyone.

She threw the phone down on the bed to charge, and sat down, knocking the coat she'd slung on the bed to the floor. She picked it up and paused. Then she hefted it experimentally, biting her lip. It was heavier than usual.

Then Summer remembered – the gift. From Mrs Brathwaite at the library.

She unwrapped the paper, which had geometric patterns in gold on it. Inside was a book, which she turned over. An old book, leatherbound. *The Journal of English Folklore Research, 1865, Volume III.*

Summer let the book fall open and realized there was a bookmark inside it, advertising a local panto from five years ago. The page where the bookmark had been slipped inside had a paragraph underlined in pencil.

Wherever we encounter these gods or devils, whether chained or bound, the same explanation is given-that it keeps them under control, or prevents others from exploiting their powers for their own gain, or in the case of benign entities, prevents them from using their power entirely. For this reason the Romans kept Saturn in fetters, from which they would release him only once a year. More mysteriously, and notoriously, they also kept the real name of Rome secret so that no one might work evil on the city, for should the secret name of Rome be known, it would give their enemies the power to destroy that ancient and venerable capital. So are the names of certain spirits kept hidden, for their names can be their undoing.

Summer kept reading, but the rest was about some goddess who had something to do with willow branches, and was kept tied up with them. Summer lost the thread pretty quickly, but she thought she had absorbed the important thing: that if you knew the name of a god or a devil or a spirit, it would give you power over it. A city, even, though she'd never known that Rome had a secret name. She'd briefly studied Ancient Rome at one of her schools, and the teacher had never mentioned it.

The question was: why did Mrs Brathwaite want her to know about it?

It was a mystery Summer didn't particularly want to solve. An image floated up in her mind of the hole getting bigger.

There was a soft knock on her door. It opened, and Mrs Pattinson stood there. 'Summer. I just . . . wanted to check that you were okay.'

'Why?' said Summer.

'*Why?* Because it seemed like you might not be.'

Summer blinked. 'I'm okay,' she said.

A long pause.

'Er . . . thank you,' added Summer.

Mrs Pattinson smiled. It made her look prettier. Her eyes kind of crinkled.

'You're welcome. I heard from Mrs Johnson that you were getting quite friendly with her Ruby and the others. That's good to hear. I just want you to know, though, that I . . . that I'm here, too, if you ever want to speak to anyone. About anything.'

She smiled and shut the door softly, leaving Summer alone.

Summer felt a slightly hot stab of shame somewhere in her stomach. Something she had wondered a few times now was . . . had she given the Pattinsons enough credit? Was it possible, in fact, that she had been a bit cold towards them since she'd moved in, expecting them to be like other people she'd lived with?

She had a horrible feeling that she had. She pictured armour and swords in her mind's eye. Her life so far had required her to put them on, to hold them out, pointy end first.

Maybe she should think about lowering them a little.

Putting the book on her bedside table, Summer made a conscious decision not to think about it and what it said –

a trick that had served her well during her life in care. Things with her foster parents were getting better. Nothing was going to change instantly, but it was going in the right direction. And she was rich – with provisos – but still rich. She had friends. Everything was good.

And Aishwarya, what about her? said a little voice at the back of her mind.

She wrapped it in willow branches, and tied it down, and threw it back into a dark cave. She'd been looked after by a succession of people who didn't love her. She was like the Romans or the Ancient Greeks or whatever – she could bury anything she needed to if she thought it might protect her.

Chapter 17

At school the next day, Summer hung out in the shed with Ruby and the others, swapping numbers so she could join the group chat on her new phone. The girls didn't laugh at her outdated model – but Ruby did give her a sticker to put on it, with a skateboarding panda on.

'Your hair would look good in plaits,' said Scarlett.

'Oh. Really?' said Summer.

'Really. Here.'

Scarlett put Summer's hair into two plaits, and Ruby took some hairbands from the pocket of her cardigan and tied them at the bottom. 'You look like a cool Pippi Longstocking,' she said.

No one had ever called Summer cool before the witch came along. She liked it.

What she didn't like was when she passed Mrs Myer's

office, on the way to the photocopying machine because Miss Taylor had asked her to make copies of the Poem for the Day, and saw a woman in there with a black dress on.

Summer paused and peered round the half-open door, and there was the witch, standing talking to Mrs Myer as if that was a perfectly normal thing to do. Right there in her jacket and petticoats and boots and hat, and Summer thought of the starlings sitting on the wooden turrets and the house at the top of the slide.

The witch turned to her and smiled. She should not have been there, in that office, with its coffee machine and modern filing boxes, its piles of paperwork and its ancient computer with the big boxy monitor. She looked as out of place as if she had been painted into the room.

'Run along now,' said Mrs Myer, putting a hand on the door handle, starting to shut it.

'And don't dawdle,' said the witch, with another smile.

Then the door closed, and Summer heard Mrs Myer say that yes, they were always looking for good supply teachers.

Summer felt something go cold, right down inside her bones. As if there wasn't marrow inside them but slush, gathered on a grey winter's day and packed into the hollows of her body.

By mid-afternoon, she had almost forgotten about seeing the witch, almost pushed it to the back of her mind. She hadn't seen Aishwarya all day – it had been raining at lunchtime, so the others were not on the climbing frame in the paddock, but doing indoor play. At the end of school, though, Summer passed her as she came out of the gates, the other girls a little behind.

'Oh, hey,' said Summer.

'You walking with me?' said Aishwarya.

Summer glanced back. The other girls were just inside the gate. 'Er, no,' she said.

Aishwarya's face didn't quite fall, but something involving gravity happened to it, as if some of her muscles had suddenly been removed. Small ones.

Summer swallowed. 'I, uh, wanted to get your number, though? So I can text you? I have a phone now.'

'Lot of changes for you,' said Aishwarya. Her voice was flat. No intonation.

'Um. Yes.' Summer had her phone out. 'Can I have it? Your number?'

Aishwarya rolled her eyes. 'It's oh seven seven five—'

'Wait,' said Summer. She was tapping at her phone, trying to work out how to store a new contact. 'I don't . . .'

Aishwarya sighed. She swung her schoolbag from her shoulder, pulled out a pen and took off the cap. 'Hand.'

'What?'

'Hold out your hand.'

Summer did, and Aishwarya wrote her number on the back of it. It hurt, a little – the pen digging into Summer's skin.

'Thanks,' Summer said, but then she felt a gentle nudge on her shoulder, and the girls were round her, sweeping her in a sort of flow that was more liquid than the action of individual bodies, and the wave of it took her past the outer wall and through the school gates on to the street.

She turned back – Aishwarya was looking away, pointedly.

Summer took a breath, and put the smile back on her face, and walked with the girls, as they chattered about the big talent show on TV and whether the guy who swallowed fire was hot.

'I imagine he would be, after swallowing fire,' said Summer, and the girls laughed, and she forgot all about Aishwarya's face. Mostly.

When she got to the end of her road, though, and the

other girls had gone, she found herself hesitating. She wasn't sure she wanted to go to the house, to see the witch, to think of another wish. She didn't know why. She had friends! Money! It was the dream.

But something held her back.

She couldn't go to Mrs Cardle's or Mr Rowntree's. They would just ask her about the witch, about Sarah, or her aunt, or whoever they thought she was. The library was shut, and even if it had been open Summer wasn't sure she wanted to face Mrs Brathwaite, who had given her that strange present of the book.

After a moment, she took out her phone and fired up the messaging app.

HEY AISHWARYA. SUMMER HERE. YOU BUSY?

YES. WORKING.

WORKING? WE DON'T HAVE ANY HOMEWORK.

MAYBE *YOU* DON'T.

Summer fastened her coat against the chill in the air. Somewhere, someone was burning wood; the scent and smoke wreathed round her. She hated feeling bad about herself. Some of the kids she'd known had been very good at making her feel like that. But doing it to herself was a new sensation.

Maybe she was just doing what she'd been taught by others.

Summer bit her lip and stabbed at the screen:

LOOK I'M SORRY ABOUT THE GATES. IT'S JUST . . . FRIENDS. I'M NOT USED TO IT.

YEAH. IT SHOWS.

SORRY. CAN I COME ROUND? WOULD LIKE TO SEE YOU AND . . . TALK TO YOU.

As she typed it, Summer realized it was true.

Three dots hovered blinkingly on her phone, telling her that Aishwarya was composing a message. It seemed to take a long time.

FINE. HAVE TO MAKE DINNER THOUGH.

MAKE DINNER?

YES. FOR ME AND MY BRO. IT'S COMPLICATED. BUT COME FOR 10 MINS. I'LL SEND YOU THE ADDRESS.

I KNOW IT. WE WALKED TO YOUR HOUSE ONCE, REMEMBER?

COOL.

Summer figured that was as good as she was going to get. She shouldered her bag and turned round, walking briskly till she was at Aishwarya's house. She was about to ring the bell, but Aishwarya opened the door, and there was a glow of light and activity from the hall within. Her little brother seemed to be cleaning football boots on the hall floor; schoolbags and uniforms were thrown on the carpeted stairs, and wisps of steam came from the kitchen – as well as an incredible smell.

'Is your mum cooking?' said Summer.

'No,' said Aishwarya, stepping aside so Summer could

enter. 'I was cooking. But I'm not now. We've eaten.'

There was a door on the other side of the corridor from the stairs, and now a voice came from it. 'Who's that, *beta*?'

'A friend from school, Mum. She's not staying long.'

Summer took a small step back. 'Right.'

Aishwarya's eyes widened a little. 'No, it's not that! It's just, I'm busy. The kitchen, cleaning, you know.'

Summer eyed the door, and the kitchen, and the brother sitting on the floor. He caught her looking.

'Mum's sick,' he said quietly.

'Rahul!' said Aishwarya in a low hiss. She looked to the door, but no voice came. She grabbed Summer's arm and pulled her to the door. 'It's not . . .' she said. 'I mean . . . she is. But not, like, dying, you know?'

'Er . . .' said Summer.

'ME,' said Aishwarya, spelling out the letters. 'Chronic fatigue? That's what Mum has. It comes and goes, but at the moment . . . Well, I'm kind of in charge.'

'I had no idea,' said Summer, feeling shapes twist inside her that she didn't know her body held.

Though now she remembered Mrs Brathwaite, the librarian, talking about Aishwarya. Hadn't she said something about feeling for her, given the circumstances? And of course Summer had ignored her because all she'd cared about was the witch in the bottle. Stupid, selfish Summer.

'Why should you?' said Aishwarya. 'Anyway. You wanted to talk about something?'

They were standing in the still-open doorway.

Summer thought about this. There were things she wanted to tell Aishwarya, but how to put them into words? The witch, the book. The little things that were bothering her – like how Sarah had not, as far as Summer could tell, had any tea or cake or toast when they went round to her elderly friends' houses, even though she'd said she was hungry.

'Just wanted to say sorry, really, for being a prat at school.'

Aishwarya laughed. 'I'm giving you points just for use of the word "prat",' she said.

'It's all the old books from the library that I read. Whatever you've been cooking smells amazing, by the way. What is it?'

'Just parathas and a load of dips, simple stuff, really. But lots of it. Rahul eats like a horse.'

Rahul whinnied, from the floor, and Aishwarya smiled at him, a smile of genuine warmth. What Summer wouldn't give to have that in her life.

'I'd invite you in, but . . .'

'Your mum?'

'Yeah. I mean, she'd like you! She'd totally want you to come in. But she'd want to make a fuss of you, and then she'd be exhausted and then . . .'

Summer nodded. 'I get it. I should go, anyway. Get back before dark. My beloved parents might worry about me.'

She was being sarcastic, but Aishwarya shook her head. 'You never know,' she said. 'Your foster mum? I saw her in the head teacher's office once; the door was open. She was shouting about the kids throwing stuff at you. One of the other mums must have told her. I didn't tell you because . . . well. I don't know. We've never really talked about it.'

Huh. Summer wasn't expecting that. It didn't fit with her idea of Mrs Pattinson.

'Er, thanks,' she said. 'Good to know. I think.'

There was a pause.

'Anyway. I'll see you tomorrow, yeah?' said Aishwarya. 'Maybe we can walk home together.'

'Totally,' said Summer, and Aishwarya smiled.

They fist-bumped, only half ironically.

Summer left and walked down the little front-garden path with a smile on her face, until she turned the corner, in the gathering gloom, and there was the witch.

'Ah,' said the witch, licking her lips. '*There* you are.'

Chapter 18

Summer stopped under a street light that lit her like a search beam. The witch was in shadow in front of her, the cat, Tobias, winding round her feet, as if tying her to the ground.

'I need your third wish,' said the witch.

Summer hesitated. 'I don't think I want one,' she said.

The inside of her head was a living room, with a huge hole in it and darkness at its bottom. She thought of what Aishwarya had said about Mrs Pattinson going to complain because of other kids being mean to her. About how she had put her hand on Summer's shoulder when she thought Summer was worried about the hole.

Summer *was* worried about the hole, of course; but not for the reason Mrs Pattinson thought.

The witch laughed, but it was a skeleton laugh; no soul in it. 'We had a compact, you and I,' she said. 'You will have your third wish.'

'I have everything I need,' said Summer. But she couldn't help glancing back at Aishwarya's house.

'Liar.'

'I do!'

The witch stepped forward, her face coming out of the dark, suddenly becoming out of nothingness, like it was a screen, and all at once a smiling expression was projected on to it. 'There is something you need, deep down inside your heart, but you will not speak it,' she said.

Summer swallowed. 'If you know that, then you don't need me to tell you.'

'Oh, but I do. I need you to ask me.'

Summer didn't stop herself looking back at Aishwarya's house this time, didn't stop herself from thinking about the house where she lived, the house with the hole in it. The house that was missing something, like she was.

'I can't,' she said.

'You can,' said the witch. 'I could command you to, but I would prefer you said it unaided.'

Tobias unwound himself from her legs, and rubbed his head against Summer's foot. 'It won't hurt you to say it,' he said.

'I can'—'

'*Speak it*,' hissed the witch, and at the same time Tobias reached up with his paw and scratched Summer's ankle, hard, and she cried out.

'Speak it or I will turn my magic on you,' said the witch. 'Speak it now or for ever I will—'

'Love,' whispered Summer, and Tobias sat back, purring, and licked his paw.

'What? Speak louder.'

'Love,' said Summer, and there was rain on her cheeks, only on her cheeks, that one small place in all the street. Everywhere else was dry: the gravel, the concrete; no clouds in all the sky. A crow called somewhere.

'I want to be loved.'

'Yes,' said the witch.

'But you can't make that happen,' said Summer.

The witch smiled again and stepped back into the darkness. 'Oh, I can,' she said. 'But I will need a bigger meal. Not tea, not cake. A dinner. A dinner, for my strength.'

Summer felt that twinge of discomfort again, a kind of stitch deep inside. She couldn't let the witch see Mr Rowntree or Mrs Cardle again. To go into their houses for a short time and come out with . . . whatever she'd come out with. She thought of Mr Rowntree turning pale all of a sudden, and Mrs Cardle blinking as the teacups and spoons rattled in their saucers.

'I don't know,' she said. 'My friends are so old and—'

'Not them,' said the witch. 'They are spent.'

Summer's unease intensified. 'Then . . .'

'There must be others.'

'Only my house, and you didn't want to go in there.'

The witch sucked her teeth. 'Never,' she said. She paused. 'But we could turn round and return to the house of your friend.'

Summer flicked her eyes to Aishwarya's house. 'No, they've eaten already. And Aishwarya's mum is resting.'

'Very well,' said the witch. 'Tomorrow, then.'

Summer felt a strange stab of relief. She wasn't sure why. The witch hadn't hurt her elderly friends, after all. Had she? Summer had seen Mr Rowntree the day before, in his front garden, kneeling to plant something.

'Tomorrow,' she said.

The witch clapped her hands and was gone. Just dark air, cool on the skin.

Summer sighed. She traipsed slowly back down the road towards her house – no, not her house: the house she lived in.

Her phone beeped. She took it out of her pocket, the glow of the screen making a circle of light, and her in it.

SORRY TO BE UNWELCOMING. COME TOMORROW FOR TEA. I'LL MAKE EXTRA. AXXXX

Summer smiled and hit the home button, the light dimming from the phone, and a gleam caught her eye, to her left.

She turned, startled. Sitting on the garden wall beside her was a cat, its eyes lanterns in the night; as soon as she looked at it, it melted away to whatever lay on the other side of the wall. Summer shook her head lightly, and then there was a roar to her right.

It all happened in a jumble: Summer twisted her head and saw a white helmet, the black shape of a scooter, engine gunning, and then there was an impact that spun her round. Something tugged at her hand, and then the bike was screeching round the corner at the end of the road, and she looked down and—

—her phone was gone.

Summer closed her eyes, breath rasping, trembling. She'd heard people talking about this at school. Moped gangs, they called them. It was often kids they stole from because they were smaller, and put up less of a fight. Of course it hadn't been a gang – just one guy.

Maybe the witch told him to do it, she thought. It was an idea that came to her despite herself. Why would the witch want to take her phone, though?

The other thinking part of her thought: *To stop me talking to people in a way she can't control.*

Summer felt her eyes welling up. Her own phone, that she'd spent all that money on.

She wiped away her tears with her sleeve, angrily. Two wishes, and she'd been left with almost nothing, apart from her hair in plaits.

When she arrived at the house, the lights were on inside, and her foster parents were home. But it was a while before she went up to the door and knocked.

Chapter 19

To Summer's surprise, it was both Mr and Mrs Pattinson who opened the door, and they smiled at her, which was surprising, too. There was TV noise coming from the den down at the other end of the kitchen. The boys were watching one of their series.

'Are you all right?' said Mrs Pattinson.

Summer blinked. 'Um. Yes. Why?'

'Your eyes are red. It looks like you've been crying.'

Summer considered this. She couldn't possibly mention the witch, or the money, or the phone. Any of it, in fact. 'Just . . . girls at school,' she said.

Mr Pattinson narrowed his eyes. 'We need to speak to that head teacher again,' he said. 'This can't continue. It's—'

'No, no!' said Summer.

She felt a bit dizzy. This was all so weird. None of her

foster families had *ever* seemed to care about how she got on at school.

'It's fine. It was actually me who . . . wasn't kind.'

She thought of Aishwarya. Lies were best when they were true. That was something she'd learned in those other foster homes.

'Oh,' said Mrs Pattinson. 'Well. Did you apologize?'

Summer thought back to Aishwarya's house. 'Yes, actually.'

'Well.' Mrs Pattinson smiled. She looked nice when she smiled, Summer always thought. 'That's that, then. We're proud of you.'

'You're . . . I'm . . . sorry. What?'

'Just that we're proud of you,' said Mrs Pattinson. She turned to her husband. 'Right?'

'Oh yes,' he said. 'Takes a lot to apologize. Be the better man and all that.'

Mrs Pattinson coughed.

'Ahem. Bigger girl, that is. I mean, um—'

'We know what you mean, dear,' said his wife. 'Now. Summer. Would you come through to the kitchen? I know you like to spend the evenings in your room, but there's something we wanted to talk to you about.'

Summer nodded, inside and out. This was how it always went – the talk. About how it wasn't working out, it wasn't anyone's fault, but it was time to move on. Et cetera. One of her teachers in one of her towns had taught them the Latin for *and the rest*. Which seemed appropriate because this was the rest of her life, this conversation. She knew it so well; she knew exactly how it would go. Summer was cross with herself for having, just a moment ago, a flare of hope in her heart.

'Fine,' she said, her voice as flat and cold as a frozen puddle in winter, stones at its bottom.

Mr and Mrs Pattinson looked at each other, frowning. Then they followed her through to the kitchen. Summer sat down heavily in the chair at the far end of the table, by the doors that opened on to the garden. The darkness beyond, no moon, made them seem like doors of pure black.

Mr and Mrs Pattinson took seats opposite her, next to one another.

Summer let out a long breath and lowered her head. She wanted to say, 'Let's get this over with.'

There was a smooth sound, the shush of an object being slid over a surface, and she looked up to see Mr Pattinson pushing a small box across the table towards her. There was a blue ribbon tied round it in a bow.

'Open it,' he said.

Summer regarded it suspiciously. This wasn't how things usually went.

'What is it?' she asked.

'You'll see,' said Mrs Pattinson. Her eyes were dancing.

Summer undid the ribbon, carefully. Both adults were watching her. This was odd. Under the ribbon was a jewellery box made of some kind of polished wood. She hinged it open, clam-like, and inside was a fat cushion of some velvety black stuff, and inside that, where a ring would normally go, was a key ring.

Summer looked down at it and frowned. A little panda figurine attached to a brass ring. She remembered mentioning, in passing, that she found pandas cute. Maybe they would become like Mrs Pattinson's bears. Maybe Summer would end up with pandas on everything. Some of the girls at school did attach key rings to their book bags, to personalize them. Maybe Mr and Mrs Pattinson were thinking she'd like to do that?

'Um, thanks?' she said.

But Mr and Mrs Pattinson were still looking at her expectantly.

'I'll . . . put it on my book bag, I guess?' she said.

Mrs Pattinson smiled. 'We were thinking it might be more useful than that.'

She nudged Mr Pattinson with her elbow, and he went into the hallway and came back with something in his hand, something that caught the light.

He handed it to Summer. It was a key. A silver, ordinary Yale key.

'To go on the key ring,' he said.

Summer stared at the key ring in one hand and the key in the other. That they fitted together was both a simple fact and, somehow, stunning.

Silence for a moment.

'Mrs Brathwaite, at the library?' said Mrs Pattinson. 'She goes to our church. She said you often go there and read after school. When you're, uh, supposed to be in After-school Club, since we aren't at home to look after you. We spoke to the teachers who run the club, too – it sounds like you don't often go?'

Summer looked down. 'I'm sorry,' she said. 'It was

because of the other kids. They weren't very—'

'We know,' said Mrs Pattinson. 'We know, and it's okay. But it's also not safe for you to be wandering the town. We'd prefer it if you went to After-school Club, but if there are days you don't want to . . . Well, now you can come back here. And let yourself in.'

Summer blinked.

'You could have told us, you know, about the other kids,' said Mr Pattinson, gently. 'We'd have tried to help.'

'We felt like *such* fools when Mrs Brathwaite filled us in,' said Mrs Pattinson. 'We haven't done this before, you see, and—' She dabbed at her eye, and Mr Pattinson held her hand.

'It's yours,' said Mr Pattinson, nodding to the key. 'Let yourself in whenever you like. *Nuestro casa es su casa.* Or is it *nuestra*? Is it *nuestra*, Sue?'

'Oh, shut up, Gavin,' said Mrs Pattinson, but she was smiling.

For a moment, Summer felt a tingle in her skin, at the thing Mr Pattinson had said – and how Mrs Cardle had said something similar to the witch. But the ring and the key were taking up too much of her attention to dwell on it, and anyway it didn't really mean anything, did it? It was just an expression.

She looked down at the key. It was the first key she'd ever owned.

'Thank you,' she said.

The key was much smaller than the phone she'd lost, but it seemed heavier somehow. Summer didn't know how that could be possible.

She turned it over and over in her fingers. And then she couldn't see it any more; she couldn't make it out because everything was water, and she couldn't see it at all.

'Oh, Summer,' said Mrs Pattinson, and she came over to Summer's side of the table and put her arm round Summer, wrapping her in it and holding her tight. It was nice. Awkward, but nice. 'I'm sorry, love,' she said. 'That we didn't pay more attention.'

'That's okay,' said Summer, voice muffled by the hug. 'I'm sorry I bunked off After-school Club.'

'Oh,' said Mrs Pattinson, 'don't worry about that. I mean, maybe try to go if you can. But don't apologize. We'll speak to the school again, see what we can do to make things easier for you.'

She took a step back and let go, her hand hovering in the air near Summer's shoulder, like she was worried to touch her in case Summer might contain some kind of powerful electric charge.

Summer wiped her eyes.

'Was it too much?' Mrs Pattinson said awkwardly, glancing at the box and key. 'Wrapping it up? We didn't mean to . . .'

She looked so anxious, standing there, her hand trembling like a cornered rabbit, that Summer felt something inside her melt, from hardness into liquid. 'No. I just . . .' she said.

'Yes?' said Mrs Pattinson.

'I've just never had a key before,' she said, quietly. 'To a house.'

Both of them smiled at that. 'We can get you another key ring,' said Mr Pattinson. 'Sue said you liked pandas, but, um, we—'

'It's great,' said Summer. 'I do like pandas. Everyone likes pandas, right? It's practically the law.'

Mr Pattinson laughed.

Summer felt tears pricking at her eyes again. She wiped her cheek with her sleeve.

Mrs Pattinson was crying more, though.

'Whoa,' said Oscar, coming into the room from the den. 'Who died?'

Mrs Pattinson closed the distance between them and sighed into Summer's hair. Her breath was warm. 'Boys,' she said, and Summer could hear her eyes roll.

Summer smiled, and prised up the tightly sprung end of the brass overlapping ring with her thumbnail, and slid the key on to it. She held it tight in her hand.

Later, as she walked past the living-room door to go to bed, she could have sworn that the hole was smaller.

Chapter 20

Apparently, the hole actually *was* smaller because when Summer left the house the next morning, her school shoes and school uniform on, Mr Pattinson was standing there on the phone, looking at it – maybe a metre across now – and saying things like, 'I just don't understand it' and 'No, we just came downstairs and it was like this'.

Summer tried not to think too much about what it might mean. She walked to school with her head down, and coasted through the morning lessons in a trance of detachment, until it was time for lunch.

Summer had to admit that the shed got boring pretty quickly. Her nails were painted blue, her hair was put in plaits and her eyelids were covered with some smokey shadow, but conversation with the other girls had quickly run out. Or not so much run out, but just always the same.

Boys and clothes and music she hadn't heard of . . .

She was in a bad mood when the end of school came.

'Go ahead – I'll catch up,' she said to the girls, as they neared the school gates.

She could see Aishwarya leaning against the noticeboard that promised the return of Mrs Bailey's famous Easter Concert. Summer had heard the Reception and Year One kids practising for this event, and she was surprised it had happened once, let alone was felt to be worth repeating.

Once Ruby and the others had turned on to the road, Summer went over to Aishwarya.

'Hey,' she said.

'Hey.'

'Want to walk together?'

Aishwarya pursed her lips. 'You're not hanging with Ruby and the gang?'

'Not today.'

'Well. Okay, then. You get my text? About dinner?'

Summer felt her stomach drop. 'Oh! Yes, I did. Thank you! But then some kid on a moped stole my phone.'

'Oh my goodness,' said Aishwarya, leaning away from the noticeboard and touching Summer's arm, all trace of her coolness gone now, a wisp of smoke disappearing into the air. 'Did you tell the police?'

'Um, no,' said Summer. She was thinking of the cat's eyes, and her suspicion that the witch was, somehow, behind the taking of the phone.

Aishwarya nodded. 'Are you okay, though?'

'Yeah, yeah, totally,' said Summer. 'Actually, I was pretty upset, but then my . . . foster parents gave me a key to the house and . . . well. That's pretty cool.' Summer's treacherous breath caught in her throat, as she said this.

Aishwarya looked into her eyes for a bit longer than was comfortable, as if processing what it might mean to feel that way, about something as simple as a key. Then she nodded.

'I see,' she said. 'Well, I think I do.'

And Summer could tell that Aishwarya *did* get it, at least a bit. Because of her mum, maybe. 'Anyway,' she said, 'dinner sounds great.'

'Cool,' said Aishwarya. 'Maybe just get changed or whatever and then come over to mine for about six? It'll take me a bit of time to cook.'

'Sure,' said Summer.

They'd started walking by now and were nearly at the

corner of Summer's street. She could feel the key in her pocket, like something hot.

Aishwarya gave her a kiss on both cheeks. 'I'm practising for when I'm a model in Paris,' she said.

It was sort of a joke, but actually Summer could totally see it. Aishwarya was the kind of beautiful that made people smile, without knowing it.

'Laters!' Aishwarya added, breezily. And then she headed her own way, her bag swinging.

Summer smiled and went round the corner, and up to the house. As she drew near, she took the key out of her pocket and held it tight. She should probably attach the key ring to her bag, like the other girls. Buy little charms to hang with it. But she liked the weight of it in her pocket. And she'd need money for the charms, of course. Well, she was a millionaire, wasn't she? Though maybe she wouldn't be after the third wish. Summer wasn't quite sure how that worked.

Also, she realized, she wasn't sure she even cared about being a millionaire. She wouldn't have said this out loud, because it would have sounded cheesy, but it seemed to her that the key she'd been given was worth more than all that money, anyway.

There was a shadow across the door of the house, which was weird because it was spring and still quite light. Somewhere a blackbird was singing. But then, when Summer walked up the little path, the shadow detached itself from the wall and poured into the shape of the witch, Sarah.

'Hello, Summer,' she said.

Summer felt herself shrinking a little inside, like what happens to a slug when you put salt on it, which was something she'd seen her foster brothers do. Somehow, she'd mostly forgotten about the witch.

'Hi,' she said.

'Dinner,' said the witch.

'Sorry?'

'I said I needed dinner. Before I could grant your third wish. You suggested it yesterday, and now, which is even better, your friend has invited you. So let us go. I'm sure she will not begrudge me entry.'

'Be-what you what?'

'I'm sure she will let me into her home.'

Something tinkled in the recesses of Summer's mind, like a bell at the back of a shop. The witch waiting for Mr Rowntree to let her in.

'Right,' she said, and paused. 'Um. How do you know? About me being invited to Aishwarya's?' She found herself very much not wanting the witch to come with her.

'Ah, I have eyes everywhere,' said the witch, and at this Tobias materialized from the brickwork of the house and sat, licking himself.

Of course, Summer thought. She'd turned yesterday, after getting the text message from Aishwarya, and seen his eyes gleaming in the dark.

'We will go now. And eat. At Aishwarya's house. With her and her delightful little brother. That will give me all the energy I need.'

No, no, no, thought Summer.

'I think . . . actually . . . her mum might not want me to go, after all,' Summer said. 'I just had a text from her and—'

'Nonsense,' said the witch. 'I heard her, when you were speaking on the doorstep yesterday. She said her mother would be pleased to meet you. Would make a fuss over you. And, besides, you don't have a phone any more.'

Summer stared. *Had* the witch had something to do with the person on the moped? It was more than possible. Evidently, she had been there while Summer spoke to

159

Aishwarya, hiding in some way in the shadows. Summer was starting to feel trapped; was starting to find it hard to breathe. Her ribs a cage, getting tighter, holding in her lungs, holding them firm.

'No,' she said, quietly.

'I'm sorry?'

'No,' Summer repeated, louder this time. 'I won't go with you.'

She didn't know what the witch wanted with Aishwarya, but she remembered what it had been like, with her, having tea. Not eating the cake, not drinking the tea. But somehow, in some way, consuming something. Taking something from those lovely old people. Something that allowed her to do her magic. Something that made faces go pale, and teacups rattle on their saucers. She thought of Mr Rowntree bending down to the earth in his front garden, and of what Summer hadn't admitted to herself until this moment – that he had looked weak and stiff. Older.

And Summer knew she couldn't let it happen to Aishwarya, whatever it was.

The witch affected, briefly, an expression of sadness. 'I'm sorry, Summer,' she said, 'but you have no choice.

You have no power here.'

'This is my house,' said Summer, holding up the key.

The witch took a step back, for a second looking genuinely shaken when she saw it. But then she smiled. 'Yes. And you're outside.'

She waved her hand and Summer felt a whooshing sensation, just like when she'd turned into a bird. The front of the house suddenly loomed increasingly large, the ground rushing up towards her, and she saw all the detail of the gravel and the serrated leaves of a dandelion growing through it.

Summer looked down the long gravel path, the dandelion flower a parasol above her, the witch's leather cobbled boots as vast as cars, the door now an unmeasurable cliff rising into the vaults of the sky.

'*Ribbit*,' she said. '*Ribbit*.'

Chapter 21

Summer couldn't see herself, but she could feel herself as a frog in every aspect: in the strength of her back legs curled over themselves; in the long tongue in her mouth; in the wide-angle view from her big round eyes. In the vast scale of the witch towering over her.

'There's no one home,' said the witch from miles above, in a voice like a sonic boom. 'No one who can help you at all.'

Summer extended those legs like pistons and threw herself through the air. She landed, legs flexing to absorb the impact of the gravelled ground, and made to leap again. But something materialized on her right side, a massive clawed paw, nearly as large as her, and it slammed her spinning off the path. She tumbled, rolled and came to a stop by the wall of the house.

The hole had been getting smaller. And now this.

She looked up to see Tobias bearing down on her, the size of an elephant, mouth open and teeth bared. She jumped aside just in time as he pounced – he hit the wall, twisting; she could hear his paws scrabbling against the gravel as he reorientated his energy to follow her.

There was a rush of air. Summer triggered her frog-leg muscles again as soon as she landed, arced into flight, but Tobias was faster and more experienced. As she came down to land in a plant pot, something closed round her, hard and sharp, and she was in his needle-toothed mouth.

Summer struggled, kicking her legs desperately, but he had her tight, holding her in place, one or two teeth digging into her flesh. She twisted so that she could see, as Tobias stalked back to the witch. He looked up at the woman, and Summer looked up, too.

She had never been in a cat's mouth before. It wasn't something she was keen to repeat.

The witch looked down at her from her towering height – she was a skyscraper, a church spire. She crouched down to bring her face close to Summer's small one.

'We will go to your friend's, yes?'

Summer could feel the cat's teeth against her slimy frog skin. She knew he could close them, and that would be it. But she couldn't bring herself to answer.

'Say yes,' said the witch. 'Or I will instruct Tobias to eat you.'

'*Ribbit*,' said Summer.

The witch cocked her head to one side. 'Hmm,' she said. There was a pause.

'*Ribbit*,' said Summer again.

'It is possible,' said the witch, 'that I erred in my choice of spell.' She straightened up again. 'Tobias, let her go.'

The cat opened his mouth and tilted his head down; Summer fell out in an undignified fashion, landing squatly on the ground, her frog limbs splaying. She looked up.

The witch waved her hand again in a complicated gesture, and Summer's view became a time-lapse video. Everything around her got smaller, shrank down to its normal dimensions, and she left the ground behind and was standing on two legs again. She swayed, unsteadily.

The witch, too, was looking unsteady. She leaned with one hand against the door frame, her skin even paler than usual, her hair suddenly loose and wild, eyes half closed. Then she turned to Summer, wincing. Tobias was licking his paws at her feet.

'I trust,' the witch said a little breathlessly, 'that you were trying to say yes?'

'Yes,' said Summer. 'Yes, okay. We'll go to Aishwarya's.'

'Excellent. After you.' The witch indicated for Summer to leave the garden.

Summer hesitated. Tobias had told on her, about the text message. But did that mean he saw *everything*? She decided to take a gamble – she hadn't seen the cat when she'd been *talking* to Aishwarya on the way home.

'Er, well, not right now. Dinner is later,' she said. 'Aishwarya has to cook. She doesn't want us until –' Aishwarya had said about six o'clock, but Summer decided, on the spur of the moment, to give herself a bit of time – 'sevenish.'

What she would do with that extra time, she didn't know yet. Maybe go and see Mrs Brathwaite? She had a feeling the librarian knew things, especially because of the book she'd given her, and Summer was now absolutely sure that this witch was hurting people, and would cause more hurt still if Summer didn't stop her.

The witch held Summer's gaze for a long time. 'Very well. I will see you at seven.'

'Um,' said Summer. 'Here or there?'

'Wherever you are,' said the witch, 'I will know, and I will find you.'

Comforting, thought Summer. 'Okay,' she said, trying to sound more confident than she felt.

The witch waved her hand, and nothing happened. She sighed. Then she turned and walked down the garden path and out on to the road. Summer had the sense, from the way the witch had sighed, that she'd wanted to disappear, dramatically, but couldn't summon the strength. That was another interesting thing to file away, in case it was useful.

Summer knew she was in a fight now, and if she lost she might die. She also knew the witch would not hesitate to kill her to get what she wanted – Summer had seen it in the woman's eyes. The ghost's eyes. That wasn't a nice thought, and it put a snowball of fear in Summer's stomach, but she didn't hide from it. She'd been in plenty of fights in her life. And sometimes she'd won. And if she lost? Well, she might have a key, and a home of sorts, but she had no family. There was no one to miss her *too* badly. She didn't want to lose, didn't want to die – but she was prepared to. In order to win and save Aishwarya.

Save the town.

The witch's footsteps faded.

Summer felt something at her feet, something warm and soft. She looked down to see Tobias gazing up at her, his green eyes luminous in the gathering dusk. He was pressing his side against her leg, then he rubbed his cheek on her trousers.

'I wouldn't have done it, you know,' said the cat.

'Sorry?'

'Eaten you,' he said. 'I don't do everything she says.'

'Oh,' said Summer. 'Er. Thanks.'

He seemed to nod, with his whiskered head, before slinking away and off down the street. But she thought she heard his voice as he went, fading from hearing.

'I don't even like frogs. . .'

Chapter 22

Summer unlocked the door and hardly even thought about the fact that it was the first time she had ever opened a door with her very own key.

She went into the living room to look at the hole.

It was bigger again. Maybe the biggest it had been – almost from one wall to the other – a yawning chasm.

That figured.

Summer needed help, and the only person she knew who *could* help was Mrs Brathwaite. The librarian wasn't here, of course, but Summer had the next best thing. She ran upstairs to the room she slept in and grabbed the book the librarian had sent her. She looked again at the page that had been marked. Now one of the lines seemed almost to vibrate off the page:

So are the names of certain spirits kept hidden, for their names can be their undoing.

Summer remembered that first conversation, when she had discovered the witch's name. Or rather she hadn't. What had she said precisely? 'You can call me Sarah.' Something like that. Not that her *name* was Sarah.

In fact, it probably wasn't her name at all. It was very likely she was hiding her true name.

Summer sat for a moment on the bed. Her heart was beating fast. She knew she didn't have much time, but this was important. Names had power: that was something Summer had known for a very long time. It was why she kept the name her mother had given her locked safely inside her heart. And the book Mrs Brathwaite had sent confirmed this. Would it give Summer leverage over the witch if she knew her true name? Assuming she had a true name, and that it was hidden?

But how could Summer possibly find out the name of a witch from centuries ago?

How did you find things out? Historical things, names, records?

You went to the library.

Summer picked up the book, put it into her rucksack and slung it over her shoulder. Then she went down the stairs, more slowly this time. She also had to warn Aishwarya, though. There was a phone in the utility room that no one ever used; generally, it just gathered voicemails from people trying to sell things.

Now Summer lifted her hand, hoping and hoping and—

—yes. There it was, a little faded but visible. Aishwarya's number written on her skin. Lucky it had been an indelible pen. She lifted the handset and dialled.

'Hi, this is the Banerjees,' said Aishwarya's voice.

'Aishwarya! It's Summer.'

'Oh, hi! You still coming?'

'I don't know,' said Summer. 'Maybe. I mean, yes, I hope so. But listen, Aishwarya.'

'Yeah?'

Summer took a breath. This was going to sound so weird; there was just no way of avoiding it. She was remembering when she and the witch went to Mr Rowntree's, and Mrs Cardle's, too. How the witch had stood on the threshold until invited in. What had she said, about going for dinner at Aishwarya's? *She will not be-something me entry.* Begrudge? Summer also remembered how each time, once they were inside, the witch had asked questions, asked for sugar or whatever, until those people told her to make herself at home.

Make yourself at home.

Summer thought that those words, like names, probably had power, too.

They must allow the witch to . . . do something. Though what it was, Summer still didn't know. She just thought it was probably bad.

'Summer?'

Aishwarya's voice on the other end of the line.

'Sorry. So it's . . . Right. A woman might come to your door, okay? If she does, and I'm not there yet, just . . . don't let her in. Wait for me. I might be a bit late. But I'm coming.'

'What?' said Aishwarya. 'Summer, this is . . .'

'Do you trust me?' said Summer.

'I . . . yeah, I guess so.'

'Then listen, please. Just don't let her in, okay? I'm on my way, but I have to stop at the library first.'

'The library? It's shutting in, like, five minutes.'

Summer looked at the clock on the wall. She had to hurry. 'There's something else,' she said.

'What?'

'If she does come in. The woman? She might try to get you to say . . . I don't know, *make yourself at home*. Or *help yourself*. Or –' Summer remembered Mrs Cardle – '*mi casa es su casa* or something. I think those phrases are sort of like spells. Whatever you do, don't say them. Tell your mum, too.'

'My mum? She'd think I was crazy. And I've gotta say, Summer, I kinda—'

'I know, I know, but just trust me, okay?'

'Summer,' said Aishwarya in a small voice. 'You're scaring me a bit.'

'Good,' said Summer, and hung up the phone.

She left the utility room and walked past the door to the living room. Her gaze was pulled towards the inescapable gaping vacancy in the middle of the floor, cordoned off with tape. The hole was like a wide, cavernous eye, regarding her blankly. She shivered.

In the front garden, Summer went behind the recycling bins and put something into her bag. As she straightened up to leave, Oscar was coming up the driveway.

'Oh, hey, Summer,' he said. 'I'm just back from football practice. Do you want to play some—'

'Another time,' said Summer. 'I have to do something.'

'Yeah, yeah, sure,' he said, looking slightly perplexed.

But she had no time to explain. She hurried down the path and on to the pavement.

She turned right, towards the high street, and that was when she saw the blue lights flashing on the roof of the ambulance outside Mrs Cardle's little cottage.

Chapter 23

Summer ran, panting, and reached Mrs Cardle's house just as a man and a woman in green uniforms were wheeling the old lady out on a stretcher.

'What happened?' she said, as she slowed to a stop.

'Sorry, miss,' said the man, raising a hand. 'I'm going to have to ask you to move away. We need to get into the—'

'It's all right,' said Mrs Cardle in a small voice, from the stretcher. 'That's Summer. She's a friend.'

'We still need to take you to A&E,' said the woman. 'You've had a minor heart attack, and you'll have to be assessed.'

Summer could see, now, the oxygen tube snaking from Mrs Cardle's nose. Her elderly friend was very white, her hair spread on the thin pillow, little hands clasped together on her chest.

'What happened?' Summer asked.

'I stood up, and then I was on the ground,' said Mrs Cardle. 'Luckily, I had my phone in my dressing-gown pocket. My daughter gave it to me for Christmas. Big buttons.'

The paramedics were opening the back doors of the ambulance and lowering a ramp for the wheeled bed. The man gave Summer a look that mingled impatience with a smile – as if to say *sorry for being a bit abrupt, but basically you do still need to go away.*

'I'm so sorry,' said Summer, partly to him, but mostly to Mrs Cardle.

'Not your fault, dear,' said Mrs Cardle. 'It's my age! Can't be helped. We're dropping like flies in this town. Won't be anyone left for the next cribbage evening at the church. Least I had a phone, unlike poor Mr Rowntree.'

They were wheeling her in and up, now.

Summer stood very still: a girl of marble, the flow of her hair and wrinkles of her clothes merely clever manipulations of stone.

'What?' she said, eventually.

The man stepped back out to begin raising the ramp.

'Mr Rowntree,' said Mrs Cardle. 'I thought you'd know,

you two being friends and all.'

Summer was on the ramp, and the woman paramedic was glaring at her, but she didn't care.

'Know what?'

'Keeled over, right in his front garden,' said Mrs Cardle. 'Stroke, apparently. They only found out when some kids walked past to go to the play park on the rec. They went home and called an ambulance.'

'Is he . . . is he . . .'

'Dead? Oh no, dear. He's recuperating, as they say. May not regain the full use of his legs, but they say he'll speak again, and he's already blinking yes and no, according to the vicar, so fingers crossed. Well. There but for the grace of God.'

'I'm sorry,' said Summer again, but probably too softly to be heard, and anyway the paramedic woman was gently yet firmly pushing her off the ramp, and then it was closing with a pneumatic hiss, and the man began to shut the doors.

'I'm sure you can visit,' he said in a not-unkind voice. 'Saint Stephen's. If you call, they'll give you the hours.'

'Thanks,' said Summer.

She stood, unmoving, as the paramedics got in, and the engine started, and the ambulance pulled away, siren wailing.

Summer stood for what might have been a minute – or an hour.

Then she rubbed her eyes. Well, now she knew what happened when the witch came round for tea. When she was hungry and needed energy for her spells. There was a feeling deep in Summer's stomach that she'd only started having since the witch turned up.

Guilt. And shame, which was a hot liquid encircling the weight of the guilt.

This was all her fault.

All her fault for making those stupid wishes.

Then, strangely, Summer's foot lifted itself up and moved a little further down the pavement. Her other foot followed it.

There was someone who could still be saved, wasn't there? Someone younger and stronger, someone the witch wanted, to give her the power to grant Summer's last, most selfish wish, her wish to be loved.

Aishwarya.

Clutching the book Mrs Brathwaite had given her, Summer kept her feet going, one after the other, and let them guide her towards the library.

Chapter 24

Mrs Brathwaite was locking the door of the library when Summer came down the high street, but she opened it again when she saw her.

'You'd better come in,' she said.

Summer followed her through the open door. She reached into her rucksack and held up the book. 'You knew I was in trouble?' she said.

'Well,' said Mrs Brathwaite, 'you more or less told me the other day.'

'You knew about the witch?'

'It was pretty clear from the questions you were asking,' said the librarian.

She sat down in one of the two small armchairs in the children's book section, and motioned for Summer to sit in the facing one.

'So . . .' said Summer. 'What do I do?'

'You opened the bottle,' said Mrs Brathwaite. It wasn't a question.

'Yes,' said Summer. And she told Mrs Brathwaite the whole story. The librarian seemed particularly interested in the sword.

'It was in a stone?' she said when Summer got to that part. 'Like in the King Arthur stories?'

'Yes,' said Summer.

'Interesting,' said Mrs Brathwaite.

'Why?'

'Points to something older than witches,' said Mrs Brathwaite.

Summer didn't know what that meant, and anyway, the rest of the story wanted to come out, so she let it, and then, when she was finished, she sat back and sighed out a long breath.

'So now the witch is out,' she said, 'and it's all my fault, and I can't put her back in again.'

'Indeed,' said Mrs Brathwaite. 'You are, as they say, on the horns of a dilemma. There are only two bad choices now.'

'*Two?*'

'Indeed. Either you leave her out, to wreak chaos, or you put her back in.'

'And . . . that would be bad? Putting her back in?'

The librarian peered at Summer. 'You feel comfortable, do you, imprisoning a woman for ever? This is why it's better not to open the bottle.'

'*Is it really?*' said Summer, sarcastically. 'I know that now, but the point is I did. So what do I do now?'

Mrs Brathwaite pointed to the book. 'What do *you* think?'

'I think . . . I need to find out her name.'

Mrs Brathwaite nodded.

'But . . . how?'

'Have you asked her?'

Summer shook her head. 'She told Mr Rowntree he could call her Sarah. But I don't think it's her name, and I don't see why she'd tell me, anyway, if it would help me.'

'Indeed.'

'So . . . ? What do I do?'

Mrs Brathwaite folded her hands. 'I couldn't possibly tell you.'

'Oh great,' said Summer, starting to stand.

'I said I couldn't tell you. I didn't say I wouldn't *help* you. The first rule of research is: start with what you know. You found a bottle with a witch in it, correct? And you have spoken to her.'

'Yes.'

'Then she may have told you something useful. It's hard for people to lie all the time. Even witches. We need to establish who she is, who she was. Something she said to you may help with that. Or she might have *not* said something, or behaved oddly, or . . . any number of things. Let's start with her. Is there anything else she told you?'

'She said she was –' Summer searched for the word – 'a found-something?'

'A foundling?'

'Yes.'

'Ah good!' Mrs Brathwaite clapped her hands together, eyes shining. 'Very good,' she said. 'Come.' Mrs Brathwaite stood and went over to her desk where she tapped at the computer keyboard and lifted the glasses that were on a chain round her neck, placing them on her nose.

'Why is that good?' said Summer, following her.

'The parish kept a record of all foundlings,' said Mrs

Brathwaite. 'Before social services and so on. Though of course we may need just a little more to go on . . . But we could start with the name Sarah, just on the off chance.'

'Okay,' said Summer. She leaned on the counter opposite Mrs Brathwaite.

'Oh, my dear,' said Mrs Brathwaite, beckoning her over. 'You may as well come this side, with me. You're not an ordinary customer.'

Summer smiled and skirted the desk till she was next to Mrs Brathwaite. She felt safe, standing there. The librarian smelled faintly of cookies, and some kind of soap. Clean, good smells. Summer didn't know what it was like to have a grandmother, but she imagined it would be something like this.

'Here,' said Mrs Brathwaite, pointing to a scan of a parish record page, handwritten in crabbed, old-fashioned handwriting. 'There was a phase when they always used the surname Parish . . . Jane Parish . . . John Parish . . . No Sarahs, though. We may have to go back a little further. They got very into Latinate names in Victorian times. All those Venetias and Victorias.'

'And these were abandoned babies, right?' said Summer.

There were more than she would have expected, more than she liked to see. It made her think of herself, and that there was another connection between her and the witch.

'Oh yes. Usually left on the church step. And, in fact . . . yes.' The librarian clicked to another screen. 'Round here, especially earlier on, in the seventeenth and eighteenth centuries, there was also a vogue for using the place where the baby was born. Peter Church, for someone left on the step, and so on. You'd get Porch, too. See here? Eleanor Porch.'

An itch, in a corner of Summer's mind. 'That's . . .'

Mrs Brathwaite turned. 'What?' She inspected Summer. 'You've thought of something. I can almost see the cogs turning in your head.'

'No . . . that is . . . I thought I had. But maybe not.'

'Hmm,' said Mrs Brathwaite. She scrolled down the scanned document. 'I can't see a Sarah . . .'

'Stop,' said Summer.

Mrs Brathwaite stopped, the mouse cursor blinking whitely. The name almost pulsed on the blueish screen as Summer looked at it.

1688. Female.

'Which one?' said Mrs Brathwaite.

Summer touched the screen – she almost felt like it might sting her, or bite, but it was only smooth and hard and slightly warm. 'Here. Mary Lane.'

'*Found on St Mary Lane, Midwinter's Day,*' read Mrs Brathwaite. 'Isn't that . . . ?'

'It's an alleyway,' said Summer. 'It runs up to the rec. But, when I wanted to go that way, Sarah – the witch, I mean – she wouldn't. She went all quiet and upset.'

'Ah,' said Mrs Brathwaite. 'Compelling. Perhaps she didn't want to risk you saying the name of the lane out loud. Or perhaps even going into the lane would have weakened her somehow.'

'She didn't want to go into the – I mean, into *my* house, either,' said Summer. 'She said she lived there once.'

Mrs Brathwaite nodded, as if this confirmed something. She turned back to the screen. 'Let me just . . .'

She pulled up another search panel and typed in 'Mary Lane', and a date range, and then—

'Ah yes. Drowned as a witch in the pond at Ducklington, 1711. Poor girl.'

'That *poor girl* has put Mrs Cardle and Mr Rowntree

in the hospital,' said Summer. 'And now she's coming for Aishwarya.'

The librarian looked up and lowered her glasses. 'That was her doing? I did wonder. Knowing you were friends and all.'

Summer swallowed hard. 'Yeah. I . . .' A treacherous tear trickled down her cheek.

Unexpectedly, Mrs Brathwaite stood and pulled her into a hug. 'Not your fault. You were curious – and lonely – and you did what anyone would have done, what many have done, in your situation.'

There was something in her tone. Still breathing in the woman's cookie smell, Summer rubbed her eyes with her free hand. 'This happened to you, too?'

Mrs Brathwaite stood back and tapped her nose. 'Not quite. But similar.'

Summer took in the gleam in her eyes, the surprising strength when the librarian had hugged her. 'And . . . you won? I mean, you defeated the witch?'

She was thinking of Aishwarya. She would not let her friend be hurt, no matter what it cost her.

'Oh yes,' said Mrs Brathwaite. 'And so will you.' She

sighed. 'Still, I do pity her. After all, it was rarely men that they drowned. Go easy on her when you do win.'

Summer nodded – then remembered Aishwarya. 'I'd better go,' she said.

'I know, child,' said Mrs Brathwaite. She put a hand either side of Summer's head, gently, and kissed her on the forehead. It tingled. 'Bless you. And keep safe.'

Summer stood there, startled, for a moment. She'd had her first hug, from Mrs Pattinson, and now her first kiss, in many years, and she almost didn't know what to do with them, like they were gifts too large to hold, or to find a place to put them down.

'Do I just . . . say her name and tell her to go away?'

Mrs Brathwaite shook her head. 'That part you have to figure out on your own.'

Summer hesitated. 'But—'

'Go,' said Mrs Brathwaite, half strict and half kind. 'There's no time to waste.'

Summer did turn, then, and began to leave. 'Thank you,' she said, as she passed the desk. 'Thank you for everything.'

'Thank me when Mary Lane is gone,' said Mrs Brathwaite. 'And I'll thank you, too, because from what I have felt of that woman I do *not* want her in this town. I have enough to contend with, training up the volunteer librarians.'

Mrs Brathwaite winked and turned to a pile of papers, and Summer knew she couldn't put if off any longer.

She had to go to Aishwarya's and face Mary Lane.

Chapter 25

Aishwarya opened the door, and Summer stood on the step for a moment.

'Is she here?' she asked.

'The woman you called me about? No.'

Summer felt a flower of relief unfurl deep down in her stomach. She went in. Aishwarya led the way to the kitchen, where she was already laying plates at the table. Her little brother was helping her, setting out sweet chilli sauce and water glasses.

'Hi, Aishwarya's friend,' he said.

'Hi, Rahul,' said Summer.

'You remember my name?'

'I'm good with names,' said Summer.

She'd had to be, with all those different houses, all those different foster parents and children. Now she also thought:

Mary Lane. That was a name she'd never forget.

'Watch out,' said Aishwarya. She edged round Summer to put a large plate of thin flatbreads in the middle of the table. There were little bowls of dip arranged round it. 'Right. Pretty much done. Rahul, is Mum in her room?'

'I think so,' said Rahul.

'Mum?' called Aishwarya.

But then Summer heard Aishwarya's mum speaking, her voice coming from the hall.

'Who's she talking to?' she asked.

'Don't know,' said Aishwarya. 'Delivery person or something? Or . . .'

But Summer was moving, towards the hallway, and she got there just as Aishwarya's mum said: 'Please, come in – the more the merrier. Summer's already here.'

The witch stepped in, over the threshold, and smiled a thin smile at Summer. Aishwarya turned to her and opened her mouth to speak, but Summer shook her head.

'Hello, *Sarah*,' she said.

The witch's smile stilled, went stiff, like plasticine left to harden and dry out. 'You can call me Mum – I've told you,' she said. She turned to Aishwarya's mother. 'Foster child,

Nick Lake

you understand. We're trying our best, aren't we, Summer?'

Summer stared at her. 'Whatever,' she said.

Aishwarya's mother shut the door and tapped her hands together, nervously. 'Girls of this age . . .' she said, vaguely.

'Do you have somewhere I can hang my coat?' asked the witch.

'Please,' said Aishwarya's mother, pointing to colourful hooks set into the understairs cupboard. 'Make yourself at—'

Aishwarya caught Summer's eye and stepped forward. 'I'll do it,' she said, and the witch glared at her, but handed over the coat.

'Come,' said Aishwarya's mother, though it wasn't quite clear who she was addressing. Maybe everyone. 'You must be hungry. Let's eat. My daughter is an excellent cook. I would do it myself, but—'

'No need to explain,' said the witch. 'Summer has told me everything.'

Aishwarya's mother gave Summer an odd look. Then she turned back to the witch. 'I'm glad Aishwarya has such friends,' she said. 'I've been worrying . . .'

'Well, she has me,' said Summer, without realizing she

was going to speak.

Aishwarya smiled at her.

'Sarah . . . Mum . . . could we speak outside for a moment?' said Summer.

'Oh, it's cold out there, dear,' said the witch. She didn't move.

Summer looked at Aishwarya, and nodded her head towards the kitchen. Aishwarya nodded back and put a hand on her mum's arm.

'Let's go sit,' she said. 'I think Rahul has had most of the parathas already. Summer and her . . . foster mother can follow us through.'

Aishwarya's mother looked uncertain for a moment, but Summer smiled at her.

'A couple of minutes,' she said. 'Just need to catch up with my . . . with Sarah.'

Aishwarya and her mother left Summer in the hallway, with the witch.

'You can't stop this,' said the witch when they were alone. 'Not any more.'

'Really?' said Summer.

'Yes. Yes, Summer. We will go through, Summer, and we

will eat. Both of us. You will eat the food your friend has cooked. And I will eat, too, and then I will have the power I need.'

'To grant my wish?'

'What?' The witch blinked. 'Oh yes. Of course.'

'I don't want my wish, though,' said Summer.

'Well, Summer, you don't have any choice. Let's go through for dinner, Summer.'

Summer took her rucksack off her back and opened it. 'You keep saying that. *Summer.* You say it like you think it's my name.'

The witch's eyes narrowed and seemed to change and darken, from hazel to moss green to the colour of a stream in winter, running through muddy ground. 'It is your name,' she said.

'Nope,' said Summer. 'It's the name I gave myself when I went into care. It's not the name my mother gave me. Not the name I was christened with.'

Now the witch was shaking her head. 'No, no, that can't be—'

'But it is,' said Summer, and it was.

She wasn't going to tell the witch her real name. It was hers alone. It was private, and it was between Summer and her mother, and it would always stay that way. No matter where her mother was, no matter what had become of her since. She had loved Summer once, even if she'd struggled with other things, and she had given her a name. And Summer would hold it always in the chambers of her heart, secret and unspoken.

The witch shook herself, as if there were insects on her skin she was casting off. 'Nevertheless,' she said, 'we will eat now.'

She made a gesture in the air, a little tune made of movement, fingers fluttering, and Summer felt herself walking towards the kitchen.

Her feet were moving of their own accord, but she tried opening her mouth, and it worked.

'Stop that, Mary Lane,' she said.

The witch came to a halt, her feet motionless.

'What did you say?' she said, voice trembling.

Summer turned. 'I said stop that, Mary Lane.'

The witch took a step back. 'No, no, you can't—'

'Oh, but I can,' said Summer. She took the bottle from her bag, the one the witch had been in for all those years. Her hands were shaking with fear, but she held it tight. 'It's over.'

The witch turned her head from side to side wildly,

hair swinging. Then she seemed to focus on a spot behind Summer. 'Never,' she said. 'But also . . . *now*.' She made another gesture with her hand.

'What?' said Summer.

'*Now*, Tobias.'

Pain needled into Summer's ankle, and she screamed, twisting to see the cat biting hard on the back of her leg, his furry body twisting as she pulled her foot forward by pure instinct, shaking it, trying to get him off. The bottle fell from her hand, and hit the ground – somehow it bounced rather than breaking – and she dived forward to catch it, and her hands closed round it. There was the sound of running feet, and then Rahul was in the hall.

'Er, Aishwarya's friend, Mum says are you ready for— Oh.'

He had stopped and was looking at Summer sprawled on the floor.

'Rahul, run. Get out of—'

But the witch was

faster.

The witch was

as quick as the flick of

a hose being turned on,

and she crossed the hall floor and lifted Rahul up under one arm, and she turned and went, as he yelped and shrieked.

There was the click of the door opening, and then it closed behind her.

Summer sat up.

Tobias was gone.

The witch was gone.

Rahul was gone.

Chapter 26

Summer knew where the witch would go.

Still clutching the bottle, she ran up the road and along the high street, and then turned on to Sheep Street. Street lights were coming on; the air was a cool envelope around her. She had to get to them; she had to save Rahul. He was so little; the witch had picked him up like he was a bag of shopping.

She passed the man from the phone shop, and he raised his hand, but she ignored him. She couldn't let Mary Lane go; she couldn't let her take Rahul.

Her throat was burning, her lungs filling raggedly with air. Crows scattered into the sky, cawing, as she passed the trees they were sitting in. At the corner with St Mary's Lane, she skidded on the gravel, turning without slowing.

There was nothing there.

Only hawthorns just starting to bloom with blossom, like clouds fallen from the sky. Only a blackbird that hopped away, chattering, into the shadow of a porch.

No.

No – there, crouching in the shadow, was the witch. She held Rahul tight to her.

'Help!' said Rahul. 'Help me.'

'Shh, boy,' said the witch, and it must have been a spell because he went silent.

Summer took a step forward, then glanced behind her. 'Tobias,' she said. 'Come out where I can see you and then stand still.'

The cat slunk out from the shade and stood, ears back. 'Summer,' he said. 'Or whatever you're called.'

'Summer will do,' said Summer, with a tight smile. 'Mary Lane. Come here.'

The witch stood full height and stepped out into the middle of the lane. She held Rahul in front of her, like a hostage. His eyes were very wide with fear.

The witch regarded Summer balefully over his head. 'You can't do this,' she said. 'I can't go back. I can't.'

'You have to,' said Summer. 'I should never have let you out.'

'But you did.' The witch pushed Rahul forward, as she took a step, a smile growing on her face. 'Mayhap even then you felt a kinship with me. We were both abandoned, weren't we? Left to others to bring up. Others that don't care about us.'

Summer thought about Aishwarya, about the key she'd been given, which was a real key and also an idea. 'People care about me,' she said.

'No,' said the witch. 'They say that, and then they turn on you. They'll do it eventually. They'll betray you, and you will be left cold and alone.'

As she said this, she was walking towards Summer, a hand out, her eyes glittering. Rahul, she was half dragging; he seemed weighed down with terror.

'But with my help you can destroy them before they turn traitor; make yourself queen of your world. You can be anything you want to be. You can—'

'Stop, Mary Lane,' said Summer, softly.

The witch stopped.

Summer opened the bottle. She knew the witch would keep talking if she let her, would worm and wheedle her way into Summer's confidence, and make her bitter and twisted like her.

The witch made a little gesture in the air.

Tobias rushed at Summer, hissing, and clawed at her leg, and Summer swallowed a curse as she kicked him away, then rubbed at the painful scratches. An ordinary cat would scatter, claws clattering on the floor, but Tobias, of course, wasn't an ordinary cat: Tobias was a witch's cat. He hissed and jumped up.

Luckily, Summer knew a trick with cats – when you'd been in enough foster homes, you picked up this sort of stuff. You lift them up by the scruff of the neck, and they think you're their mother; it's a sense memory they can't help, and they go all still and calm.

She reached down and seized him, quick and deft, then held him aloft. Praying this would work, even with him not being an ordinary cat.

And yes – he went still.

Holding him, she eyed Tobias warily – he was gazing at her where he dangled, with glazed eyes, back legs tucked up, kitten-like. It was almost as if she could see something in his expression – something that reminded her of when he had spoken to her kindly, after she was a frog.

Then Summer turned to the witch.

'Let go of the boy, Mary Lane,' she said.

'Very well,' said the witch, with a smile, and bent down to Rahul's level. She put a hand on his cheek.

'No!' said Summer, realizing she had not been clear enough. You had to be specific with spells; that was something she had learned from books at the library. 'Do not take anything from him. Leave him alone and let him go.'

Mary Lane hissed, standing straight. She released Rahul, and he ran to Summer and clutched at her.

'Go,' said Summer. 'Run home. Go back to Aishwarya and tell her to stay there.'

He nodded at her. She saw that his eyes were wet. Then he edged past her and ran, and she glanced round to make sure he was out of the alley and on the main street before she turned back to Mary Lane, who, of course, was creeping up on her.

'Summer,' she said in a wheedling voice. 'Summer, it doesn't have to be—'

Summer sighed. She held up the bottle.

'Mary Lane. Get into the bottle,' she said. 'Now.'

And it was as simple as that.

So simple, Summer couldn't believe it.

The witch was solid, a thing of flesh and fabric, and then she was a form made out of smoke, and then the smoke rose into the air, coiling, and flew down the lane towards Summer and narrowed until it poured into the bottle, swirling. There was a smell of distant bonfires in the air.

Summer dropped Tobias and put the cork in the bottle, and it was only then, in the quiet that ensued, that she realized the witch had been screaming, all that time.

'Well,' said Tobias, looking up from licking himself, as if nothing at all had happened, as if he hadn't tried to attack her. 'You won.'

Chapter 27

Summer looked down at the cat.

You won.

She thought back to what Mrs Brathwaite had said. 'It was rarely men that they drowned.'

Summer let out of a little scream of frustration and stamped her foot. She didn't think she'd ever stamped her foot before.

'Goodness,' said Tobias. 'You don't seem very happy about this. Is it because you forgot to capture me, too?'

'No,' said Summer. Though it was annoying to have this pointed out.

She closed her eyes for a long moment, but when she opened them she still had the same feeling. Guilt. Winged things turning in her stomach, trying to get out.

She bit her lip, and then she pulled out the stopper.

'Come out, Mary Lane,' she said. 'And stand before me.'

The smoke rose up, arced, came down in the shape of a woman.

'Yes?' said Mary, coldly.

Summer hesitated. 'It isn't right,' she said at last. 'You being in there.'

'It isn't,' said Mary. 'But what are you going to do about it? This is a fight. A question of power. And it's a fight you have won.' Her eyes, her eyes of smoke, flicked over to Tobias – but Summer held up a hand.

'No,' she said. 'No tricks, Mary Lane.'

The witch looked back at her, and all of winter was in her eyes, ice and snow and wind. Summer thought of Mrs Brathwaite saying that there were only two bad choices: to leave the witch out of the bottle or to imprison her for ever.

Was that true, though?

'I think . . .' said Summer, 'I think maybe you should move on? I mean . . . do you *have* to be . . . a ghost? Or whatever you are?'

'Move on?' said the witch. 'To where?'

Summer had forgotten the woman was over three hundred years old.

'Forgive,' she said. 'Forgive . . . everyone.' She made a circular gesture at the lane, the town.

The witch glared. 'The people of this place drowned me for nothing more than helping women who were in pain. All the time, when I was in the bottle, I felt the water enter my lungs, over and over, like breathing, but not air, only agony. I will never forgive.'

'But you were going to hurt others,' said Summer. 'You *did* hurt people. My friends. You would have hurt more. What would have happened to Aishwarya's mum? She'd have died, wouldn't she?'

'Perhaps,' said the witch. 'But they hurt me.'

'*They* didn't. People who died hundreds of years ago did.'

'I care not! People killed me; I will kill in return. It is all I have dreamed of all those long years in that bottle. All those centuries.'

Summer frowned. Something about this didn't add up. She saw, in her mind's eye, scales and fire.

'Why the dragon?' she said.

'Pardon?' said the witch.

'The dragon. I kind of assumed you put it there, but it doesn't . . . I mean, if you wanted to be free, to take your revenge or whatever, then why guard the bottle with a dragon?'

The witch gave a small laugh. 'That! With my last strength, I called it when they threw my bottle into a well, when they buried me. But not to *guard* me. Only to make me seem a treasure.'

'What?'

'Let us say you find a bottle, with instructions not to open it for it contains a witch. You would think twice, yes? But if you have to defeat a dragon . . . then you might think it a prize. Something worth having. Something worth opening. As you did.'

'But the skeletons. The sword . . .'

'Illusions. Figments.'

Summer thought back. She had turned after she'd won the bottle, and the dragon had still been there, coiled in the corner of the cave. 'And the dragon?'

'Oh, he's real,' said the witch. 'There are things in this country older than you can imagine. But I called him and bound him to me. Like Tobias.'

Summer thought of what Mrs Brathwaite had said, when she'd told her about the sword in the stone – how it pointed to something older than witches. Hadn't those been her words?

'Tobias is old?' she asked.

'Incalculably.'

Tobias rubbed his head against Summer's leg. She was getting distracted.

'So . . .' she said, 'if you . . . left, then the dragon would be free. Tobias would be free.'

'Yes.'

Tobias looked up at Summer and then swiftly away.

'And you would be free,' continued Summer, turning back to the witch.

'N-no,' said the witch.

But Summer sensed something: a catch in the woman's voice. 'I think you're tired,' she said. 'I think you don't really want to hurt people. I think you don't want to go back in the bottle, either.'

The witch, Mary Lane, raised her hands. 'It is only vengeance that is keeping me here,' she said.

'Exactly,' said Summer.

She thought of all the people who had hurt her in her life. Once, she would have wanted to hurt them back. Not any more.

Mary Lane rubbed her eyes.

Neither of them said anything.

'Sometimes,' Summer said, 'all you need is a little push.'

'I don't unders—'

Summer held up a hand. 'Mary Lane,' she said. And she said it in Mary's own voice, in the witch's voice, the vowels stretched a little further and in odder directions than present-day people pronounced them. This was a trick she knew, that she had known all her life.

'Y-yes?' said Mary.

'I command you to move on,' Summer continued, and it was still in the witch's own voice. 'To leave here and go to whatever lies on the other side of life. I command you to leave.'

She didn't know where these words came from; it was like they had been born in her mouth.

Mary Lane's eyes filled with tears, and Summer didn't know how that was possible, for a ghost to cry.

'*Thank you,*' the witch whispered.

Then she rose, but this time not as smoke. This time her body frayed at the edges, became smudges and motes of darkness, which fluttered apart, drifting up between the buildings of the lane. It floated past the overhanging window

of a medieval house and its black beams, and then she was no longer a woman, she was birds. Hundreds of birds surged up, a chimney of beating wings, and then spread out as they left the eaves and roofs behind, curled into the sky a flock, flying, wings beating, calling.

The flock turned in a slow circle – and then they were gone.

Starlings.

Starlings winking out of existence, far away in the deep blue sky. A hundred of them, a thousand.

Summer looked down at Tobias. 'Don't say anything,' she said.

He shook his head.

She hadn't known a cat could cry, either.

Chapter 28

Summer waved to her foster parents and hurried into the utility room.

She hit redial, hoping, and yes—

'Hi,' said Aishwarya. 'Aishwarya Banerjee speak—'

'Hi,' said Summer, hurriedly. 'Listen, Ash, I'm so sorry. I had no idea that—'

'That you'd be this late? I mean, come on.' Aishwarya was laughing, though. 'If you hurry, you might get, like, one paratha. But my little brother eats like a pig.'

'What?'

'A pig. He stuffs himself. He's—'

'No, I mean your brother is there?'

'Yeah, why?'

'I thought I saw him on Sheep Street.'

'Er . . .' said Aishwarya. 'Oh yes! He had to go out. An

errand, I think . . . Actually, I'm not . . . I think . . . Huh. I'm not sure what . . .' There was the sound of a hand going over the receiver, a rustling noise. 'Rahul! Where did you go again? Before dinner.'

A murmur, from somewhere on the other end of the line.

'What did he say?' said Summer.

'He doesn't remember, either,' said Aishwarya. 'Anyway. You coming?'

They didn't remember.

Summer smiled.

'Yeah,' she said, 'I'm coming.'

Chapter 29

On the way out of the house, Summer opened the living-room door.

Slowly, she craned her head round.

The hole was still there. But a lot smaller now.

'What are you doing?' asked Mr Pattinson, and Summer startled, banging her wrist on the door. Pain shivered down her arm. Very real. Very there. Very present. Like the hole. For a moment, with Rahul and Aishwarya forgetting, she had wondered if this had all been a dream. Clearly not.

'Checking the hole was still there,' said Summer.

'Hardly likely to have moved on its own,' said Mr Pattinson. 'Big great hole like that. Though actually, it's definitely smaller than it was before. Still. The point remains.'

'Right,' said Summer.

'You could fill it in if you like,' he said. 'Earn some pocket money.'

'I don't know if I could—'

'I'm joking!' he said. 'Honestly. You're no more than a slip of a girl.'

'Hey,' said Mrs Pattinson, walking past, carrying a book. 'Girls can do anything, you know. Especially Summer. I get the feeling Summer is pretty tough.' She smiled and patted Summer's arm.

Yes, thought Summer. *Yes, maybe I am.*

It was a nice feeling. The pat on the arm; the affection. But also the feeling inside, of what she could do if she set her mind to it.

It was new, all of it: and it was nice.

Chapter 30

'Bloody hell fire,' said Aishwarya. 'No wonder you've been weird lately.'

It was the next day. They'd had an amazing dinner at Aishwarya's the night before – a little cold, but Summer hadn't minded. Now they were on their way home from school, and Summer had told Aishwarya everything. The whole story, including the witch turning up at Aishwarya's house, which Aishwarya didn't remember – though it didn't seem to stop her believing Summer.

Summer stopped for a moment, at the corner of her street. '*Bloody hell fire?*' she said.

Aishwarya rolled her eyes. 'It's something my gran used to say. Seemed appropriate. Anyway, you can't talk, Miss Archaic Expressions. You once told me that I was "a brick" for lending you my coat.'

''S not my fault,' said Summer. 'Comes from learning

stuff from books, not people.'

Aishwarya nodded. 'Not that you could get *this* from books. Witches, and bottles, and dragons. Is the dragon still there, by the way?'

Summer blinked. 'Oh. I don't know.' She hadn't thought of this. 'It might be.'

'What about the hole?'

'Being filled in next week. Easier now it's smaller, apparently. Builders are coming. Mr – I mean, my foster father, he sorted it with the insurance in the end. They're paying half or something.'

'And the cat? Thomas?'

'Tobias.'

'He's just . . . gone?'

'Yeah. I kind of . . . walked home in a daze after the lane, after the witch . . . Mary, I should say . . . after Mary turned into birds. When I remembered about him, I realized he wasn't there.'

'I wouldn't believe you, but . . . having seen that cash balance . . .'

They'd gone to the bank, and Summer had put in her card – the money was still there. Millions. And then, as she and Aishwarya watched, the numbers had begun to blur and move, in a way that no numbers on a bank machine should do, and they had ticked down to zero, right in front of their eyes, rolling down to nothing, as if the money had never been there.

'Whoa,' Aishwarya had said. 'Did you see that?'

And Summer had nodded. The witch's magic was disappearing, erasing itself, just as she had disappeared herself, into birds and sky.

'Does this mean the other girls are going to stop fawning over you, too?' Aishwarya had said.

'I guess so,' Summer had replied.

'Oh well,' Aishwarya had said. 'I'll still be your first friend.'

Summer was still thinking about that as they drew level with her house.

Her house.

She only just realized, right then and at that moment, that this was how it appeared to her in her mind, this was what she had let herself call it.

Her house.

'So I guess things go back to normal now?' said Aishwarya. 'Or better than normal, really?'

'What?' said Summer, who had been thinking about houses, and how they could suddenly become yours.

'I mean, you'll use your shiny new key to come home – you won't have to hang out all the time at the library, or with Mrs Cardle or Mr Rowntree . . .'

'I didn't know you knew about that,' said Summer.

'You're not the only one who hangs out with old people and librarians. We're both geeks.'

'Ha,' said Summer. 'Well, I'm not going to stop hanging out with Mrs Cardle or Mr Rowntree just because I have a home to go to now. When they get out of hospital, anyway. They're my friends.'

She'd called the hospital – it was one of the first things she'd done. Both of Summer's elderly friends had made good recoveries and were coming home soon. 'Near-miraculous recovery', in fact, was what the nurse had said about Mr Rowntree. Summer wondered if maybe it *was* a kind of miracle. If the witch going had undone something.

She also wondered if the witch, in the first place, had never meant the old people to die. If she had taken only what she needed and no more. Summer supposed she would never know.

Now she looked at Aishwarya.

'Actually . . .' Summer said.

'Yeah?'

'I was thinking that after school I might start doing something different.'

'Like?'

'Well, I thought . . . I might . . . sometimes . . . come to your house and help out. With your mum and stuff.'

Aishwarya's eyes lit, like car lights coming on. 'I'd like that,' she said.

Summer felt a slight pang of guilt, at the part she hadn't told Aishwarya. About what had happened to her little brother – or nearly happened.

'You coming round today, then?' said Aishwarya.

'Not today,' said Summer, her hand on the gate. 'I thought I should . . . be here a bit. Get to know them. I know that sounds weird.'

'It doesn't,' said Aishwarya.

'Cool,' said Summer.

For a moment, there was a faintly awkward silence, then Aishwarya turned to go. But she stopped just past the front garden.

'Why did you do it?' she said. 'The . . . the wishes and stuff? Especially the last one, when you had already kind of guessed what the witch was doing.'

Summer felt a leap in her chest; a fish in there, flipping over.

'I just wanted . . .'

'Yeah?'

'I wanted . . .'

She thought back to when the dragon had said what it said, about treasure not looking like treasure. She was just going to say it. She was just going to let it out of her mouth. The words. Put them into the world.

'I just wanted to hear someone say that they love me,' she said all in a rush.

And there it was.

Spoken.

Impossible to take back.

Aishwarya looked at her with wonder, with surprise, with something else – something Summer didn't even dare to think – in her eyes.

'But *I* love you, silly,' she said. 'You're my best friend. Didn't you know that?'

And then she smiled, almost as if she'd engineered the whole conversation, carved the whole thing towards this moment, allowing those words to float over the air to Summer. And then she turned back again in the direction of her house, and she really did leave – which was a good thing.

Because Summer didn't want her friend to see her cry.

Chapter 31

Summer wiped away her tears with the back of her hand, and took a step towards the door, and almost tripped over something that was on the path; something firm and yet soft.

'Watch it, clumsy,' said Tobias.

Summer looked down at him. 'What are you doing here?' she said. She'd half expected him to be gone, like the money. But he was old. The witch had said that.

'What am I supposed to do?' said Tobias. 'Hunt for mice on a farm? I'm a witch's cat.'

'So find a witch,' said Summer.

He looked up at her, pointedly, and then at the door.

'I'm not a witch,' she said. 'I don't have any . . . magical powers or whatever. I can't do spells.'

Tobias licked his paw. 'Really?' he said. 'You, who speaks in the voice of others?'

Summer opened her mouth to say something. Then closed it again.

'So . . . what . . . you want to live here?'

'Oh yes, please,' said Tobias. 'If you'll have me.'

'It's not really up to me,' said Summer. 'It's up to my . . . to my foster parents.'

She indicated the house – the family were home; she could see Mrs Pattinson walking into the kitchen and hear her shouting something to one of the boys about homework.

'So ask them,' said Tobias.

Summer thought about this. A talking cat? She could think of worse things. And especially one who could make himself invisible and who knew what else.

'Okay. But they might say no.'

'You can hold me if you like. It will make me seem unthreatening and sweet.'

'*Seem?*'

'Well, I am a witch's cat.'

'You might also want to, you know, *not talk*,' said Summer. 'If you want to seem unthreatening.'

The cat rolled his eyes, which she hadn't known a cat

could do. 'I am aware,' he said.

She stooped down, and he leaped into her arms and fitted there surprisingly nicely. She had to open the door handle with one hand, which was a little awkward, but she managed it. Inside, Mrs Pattinson poked her head out of the kitchen.

'Hi, Summer, and— Oh! Who's that?'

Mr Pattinson came out of his office, looking curious. 'Who's what?'

'The cat.'

'What cat?'

Summer held up Tobias, and the two foster parents stared at him.

'We, um, don't have a cat,' said Mr Pattinson, unnecessarily.

'He's, um, in need of a loving home,' said Summer. It was a phrase people had used about her.

Mr Pattinson looked sceptical. 'Is he tagged? He might belong to someone else. We can't just take in any stray.'

'*Gavin,*' said Mrs Pattinson, nudging him – quite hard – with her elbow.

'What?' He looked at Summer and went a bit red. 'Oh. Sorry, Summer. No offence intended.'

'*Gavin.*'

'What?'

'It's okay,' said Summer, giggling. 'I knew what you meant. And . . .' She wasn't sure what she was going to say, and then she was. 'And don't worry, it *did* belong to someone. Mrs Brathwaite at the library? But she can't look after him any more.'

She knew somehow – she just knew – that Mrs Brathwaite would back her up on this when she told her. She'd do that after school tomorrow. She and Mrs Brathwaite had a lot to catch up on.

'Oh,' said Mrs Pattinson. 'Is Mrs B unwell? I hope she's not—'

'No, no,' said Summer. 'She's just, um, allergic.'

'She got a cat, and she's allergic to cats?' said Mr Pattinson.

'Well, she didn't know she was allergic when she got it.'

A light scratch on her hand, from Tobias. She understood. '*Him*, I mean. His name is Tobias.'

'I'm surprised Mrs Brathwaite would have taken on a cat when she has that house rabbit already,' said Mrs Pattinson.

Oh.

'Yeah . . .' said Summer. 'Maybe that was part of the problem.' She really was going to have a lot to talk to Mrs Brathwaite about. 'Anyway. Er. Can I keep him . . . ?'

Oscar stuck his head out of the living room. 'We're getting a cat? Cool!'

The Pattinson parents said nothing.

Summer stood there, a little anxious, not moving.

She stood there like a girl made of wood.

Then Mr Pattinson smiled. 'Might be nice to have a cat about the house, love?' he said to his wife.

Mrs Pattinson smiled back at him.

'Well, that settles it,' said Mr Pattinson. 'Anyway, you're not going anywhere, are you, Summer? This is your home.'

Summer blinked back *more* tears.

'We'll have to check with Mrs Brathwaite that he's got all his jabs and things,' said Mrs Pattinson. 'And what the best food is and—'

'I'll go and see her!' said Summer, hurriedly. 'When I've got him settled in.'

Mrs Pattinson nodded, approvingly. 'Very responsible.'

Summer indicated the staircase. 'I'll just take him up and show him the . . . I mean my . . . my . . .'

'Your room,' said Mr Pattinson.

'Yes,' said Summer. 'My room.'

The words felt true, for what might be the first time ever.

She set off up the stairs as her younger foster brother came out of the kitchen, eating a biscuit and looking around a little vaguely. 'What did I miss?' he said.

'A cat,' said Oscar. 'Summer's got one now.'

'Oh,' said Ethan. 'Well, I suppose we don't need a cat flap. It can go through the hole in the living room.'

'That hole doesn't go anywhere,' said Oscar.

'Bet it does,' said Ethan.

Summer smiled to herself and continued up the stairs.

In her room, Tobias looked around, seemed satisfied, then jumped up on to the bed. He turned round a few times in a patch of sunshine from the window, licked himself, then closed his eyes.

'Hmm,' he said, purring. 'There was a hole in everything. And now everything is whole.'

Then he went to sleep.

Chapter 32

Summer was half asleep and half awake. The faint green hands of the cheap alarm clock by her bed said 2 a.m.

There was a hole in everything . . .

In her dream, a cat with a monocle and a top hat kept saying that: *There was a hole in everything . . . there was a hole in everything . . .*

And then Aishwarya appeared beside him, and they were sitting at a tea table, and there were cakes laid out, a teapot with a pink knitted cosy. There was a similar one at Mrs Cardle's house.

Is the dragon still there? Aishwarya said, sipping from a cup of tea, little finger curled up.

Summer sat upright, suddenly awake.

There *was* a hole.

Not there *is* a hole.

The hole was going to be filled in.

With the dragon inside it.

She swung her legs out of bed, and Tobias, curled at her feet, stirred. 'Where are you going?' he said.

'Something to do.'

He stretched and leaped down lightly to the ground. 'Then I'm coming with you. Never know when you might need protection.'

'And you're going to protect me? You're a cat.'

'I'm not just any cat.'

'True,' she said.

Together, they went downstairs and into the living room. When they reached the hole in the floor, Summer reached down for Tobias, but he gave her a scathing look and flickered instantly out of sight, like a screen switching off. The hole was narrow now, almost too narrow for Summer to get down into it, but she just fitted, the rock scraping her skin.

When she climbed down to the bottom of the hole, Tobias was already there, licking himself casually, waiting for her.

They crawled through to the cave. Well, Summer crawled, and Tobias walked. The dragon was curled up in the corner, scales gleaming in the light of the torches, which were still somehow lit. Smoke curled from his nose. As they approached, he opened one enormous eye.

'You disturb my slumber again?' he asked, but gently this time.

'Yes,' said Summer. 'You see . . . they're going to fill in the hole. I thought you might want to get out before that.'

'I can't,' he said. 'I am under a spell.'

'No,' said Tobias. 'The witch is gone. We can both leave if we want to.'

Summer looked at the cat. He could leave, but he'd chosen to stay with her? She felt a warmth in her stomach.

'Oh, don't let it go to your head,' said Tobias, with a hiss.

'Is this true?' said the dragon to Summer.

'Yes,' she said.

The dragon breathed out fire. 'Thank you,' he said, eventually. He uncurled himself, unfolding his wings, stretching.

'Where will you go?' said Summer.

'I have a notion,' said the dragon. 'Would you like to come with me and see?'

'Come?'

'Yes. You could ride. On my back.'

Summer smiled. 'That sounds fun,' she said.

'So. Approach.'

The dragon lowered his head, flattening himself to the stone floor, and Summer came close, Tobias walking at her feet. They climbed up, from the clawed foot to the leg to the back. The dragon was warm, smooth and hard – and his scales were useful handholds to haul herself up with. Tobias actually seemed to find it more difficult, as it was quite slippery, but he scrabbled his way up, and Summer lifted him on to her lap.

'Ready?' asked the dragon.

Summer looked down at his massive bulk. 'No. But yes.'

The dragon snorted out what might have been flaming laughter. Then he propelled himself forward, half running, half flapping his wings, and they surged through the cave. Summer thought the tunnel would be too small, but the dragon powered his head towards it and somehow they were inside, flowing through. Then they were up through the hole in the living room, which was either much bigger, or they were much smaller, and they swooped up and round, through the living-room door into the hall. And then they definitely *were* small because they flew through the letter box and out into the street.

There, they grew again until Summer was riding a dragon the size of a house, the size of several houses, over the dark town, with its lit street lamps, and wisps of fog clinging to them and to the trees.

And they flew.

The Last Chapter

They flew over the housing estate on the outskirts of the town, and then over woods, where owls called, and on to a river, which ribboned silver as molten metal across farmland, between low hills. They passed a field of sheep sleeping under an old oak tree, and a farm, its outbuildings glowing with electric light – and then the dragon turned, and banked, curving round a small lake lined with yew trees.

Lightly, he landed by the shore. A half-moon hung above, and the water shone. A swan, startled, swam away. Rushes rose vertical from the dark shallows. There was a scent of something in the air. Like the colour green in a smell.

'I will stay here,' said the dragon.

'Here?' said Summer, looking around. She clambered down, helping Tobias on to the damp grass.

'Yes. This is a place of power. You don't feel it?'

'No.'

He inclined his head. 'See the yew trees? They always mark places like this.' Then he turned to the lake. 'See the water? It's full of swords and armour. Tribute and sacrifice. That's what she was doing there, after all, the Lady of the Lake.'

'What?'

'The Lady of the Lake. The one who gave Arthur the sword. Or gave it to him again, when he broke the one from the stone, depending on the story. You never wondered why she was there in the first place, in a lake? Because someone threw her in. Someone drowned her, like they did to your witch, and gave her endless magic. That's the price, you see. That's the part they don't expect to happen.'

'I . . . don't see. Not really.'

The dragon seemed to shrug. 'Well,' he said, 'the power is here nevertheless. Precious things, when lost, when abandoned, make magic. Like Arthur's sword.'

'Arthur wasn't real, though,' said Summer.

The dragon drew his head close, his eye level with her, the pupil a dish plate in the moonlight. 'You think that, do you?' he said.

She looked at his scaled tail curling in the thin mist by the lake, so far away from her because he was so big, then at Tobias by her feet, eyes glinting in the dim light. Pale smoke from the dragon's nostrils curled up into the night sky, into the mist, making more of it, mingling with it.

'No,' she said. 'Maybe not.'

They stood there in silence for some time.

'There's one thing I don't understand,' said Summer, eventually.

'Yes?' said the dragon.

'The witch said she called you, to make the bottle seem like treasure. But . . . why did the hole open up? In the living-room floor?'

The dragon blinked slowly. And did its mouth curl into a smile?

'The witch had power,' he said. 'But I have powers of my own. Perhaps I sensed that the right person had come.'

'The right person for what?'

His eye glinted. 'The right person to understand what the witch didn't. That the bottle *was* treasure. If only you knew what to do with it.'

Summer thought about that.

'What . . . what do I do *now*, though?' she said.

All her life, she had not belonged. She didn't know quite how to go about it. Thoughts she had always tried to keep at bay with distraction came rushing in.

'Whatever you want,' said the dragon. 'You can make your own world.'

'You don't know—'

'But I do know,' said the dragon.

'I'm nothing. My own mother didn't want me.'

This wasn't all true – Summer knew that – but it was something she often thought, anyway.

It was the last thing, she realized.

The last thing, after all this fighting and wishing, that she had to face.

The dragon breathed out fire over the lake. 'You are wrong,' he said. 'Isn't she, Tobias?'

Tobias looked up at Summer. Each of his eyes was a moon. 'Yes,' he said. 'Your mother loved you. It's all around you, like a cloak. It glows.'

Then the dragon lowered his head right down, and he breathed in, and time stopped for an instant, and he spoke to her, in her very own voice, the one she kept hidden, the one she never used, not for anyone. Her own deep accent, which was also her mother's.

And what he spoke to her was her name, her real true name, the one her mother had given her. He spoke it, and he put it into the world, but also he didn't speak it, also he breathed it, he made it breath, he made it life, he made it flames and smoke drifting over the lake. He spoke it like a question.

'Yes?' she said. Very quietly.

'Most of what is and lives has known cold,' said the dragon. Its breath was smoke. 'Has been set aside, been broken. But look at iron: you leave it in the rain and the air and it doesn't disappear; no, it turns rust; it turns golden; becomes more than it was. Same with you. You glow. You are cracked, but you have been put back together; you have been joined; you have been soldered. You are stronger than even you know.' He raised his head again. 'You are the *strongest*.'

Then he beat his wings, and the downrush of air whipped Summer's hair back from her head, and he rose into the sky, swift as a rocket, and arced there, hovering for a moment, before plunging down into the lake with a great splash and hiss.

And he was gone. The water rippled, silver.

Summer looked down at Tobias.

He looked up at her.

'Well,' he said, 'we'd better get going. It's a long walk back. And I really hope you have your key because that dragon took us through the letter box.'

Summer glanced at her pyjamas. 'Um. No.'

'Ah well,' said Tobias, 'we'll think of something. After all, I am a magic cat.'

'True,' she said. 'True. Can you magic us home, then?'

'Unfortunately,' he said, 'I'm not *that* magic. But you can carry me if you like.'

Summer laughed. Overhead, a flock of starlings swirled, like wind with wings, and she watched them go.

Then she turned and headed home.

THE END

ACKNOWLEDGEMENTS

I am indebted, for making the words of this book better, to Lucy Rogers, Lucy Pearse, Eve Ainsworth, Millie Hoskins and – as always – Hannah Lake.

Because pictures tell a lot of Summer's story, I am deeply grateful to the amazing Emily Gravett for the stunning artwork throughout, as well as to David McDougall for the elegant and beautiful design. All books are collaborative things, and this one more than most. Emily, and the whole team at Simon & Schuster, have taken a word document and turned it into something bigger; for me, merely to be associated with anything as extraordinary as the sequence in this book from pages 212 to 217 is an immense honour and privilege.

OPEN THE DOOR TO THE MOST ENTHRALLING ADVENTURE

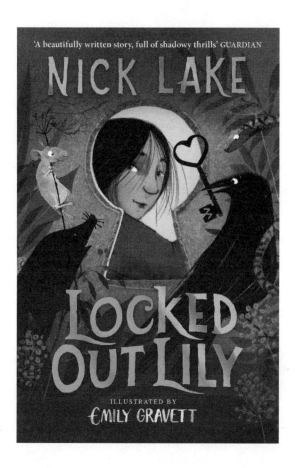

A startlingly original, stunningly-illustrated
modern classic about learning to face your fears